Pursuit of Demons

A Detective Story

D.J. Maughan

Hulyeseg Publishing

For you, boys. The first step to success is believing in yourself. I love you.

Chapter 1

Renata

December 2000, Budapest

My chest is thumping, but is it internal or external? I think it's both. The bass is so loud it reverberates in my ears. Why is techno music played so loud? Does anyone like it, or is it the Emperor's New Clothes? It's music you feel rather than hear. It doesn't move you to emotion. It rattles your teeth. Someday, we'll all lose our teeth and wish we could hear.

"What can I get you?"

The handsome man stands impatiently, strumming his fingers on the bar. His eyes glare at us. We're a nuisance to him.

Agnes turns to me. "What are you going to have?"

I glare at her. She knows I don't want anything, and she shouldn't either. She presses her mouth to my ear. "What do you want to drink?"

My frustration boils as I glare back at my best friend since childhood. I cup my hand to her ear. "Nothing! And you shouldn't either."

She pulls away and waves her hand. I shouldn't be surprised. She's always had a mind of her own and rarely listens to me. I've known it since I agreed to come: this is a mistake. Why did I let David talk me into it? We've been here fifteen minutes and still haven't seen him.

"Come on," Agnes pleads, "you'll feel better with just one drink. Promise."

That's always her thing, "Promise." She knows I've wanted to leave since we arrived. The drink is her way of getting me to stay. She thinks I'm too stiff. Since arriving in Budapest, she's been begging me to come to a club with her. This morning, when I suggested we go, I thought her smile might split her face. Little does she know I'm here for David, not her. Alcohol won't help me relax. He will. Neither she nor I have ever imbibed much alcohol, except for one time several months back. We spent hours vomiting in a toilet, promising we'd never do it again.

The bartender has lost any meager patience he's had. "Hey! Look, I don't have time for you stupid girls. Look at all the other people waiting. Come back when you know what you want, and stop wasting everyone's time."

He glares at us, daring us to say something. His look only amplifies my anxiety. We shouldn't have come here. Not just here, Budapest in general.

We stare back at him, mouths agape. We aren't accustomed to being talked to like this. An arm wraps around my shoulder. I glance in the direction of the arm and see a familiar hand.

"That's no way to talk to these beautiful ladies. A little more respect would be appreciated."

I turn toward the voice, craning my neck up to see. David isn't looking at me. His steely eyes are fixed on the bartender. My knees go weak as he embraces me. He turns in my direction, and I melt. Like always, his dark hair is perfectly manicured. A smile plays at the corners of his mouth before he turns his gaze back to the bartender.

I force my eyes away from his handsome face.

The bartender has become apologetic. "I'm sorry, ladies... it's just a busy night. Did you decide what you'd like to have?" He forces a smile.

We hesitate, looking back and forth from the bartender to David. We say nothing, forcing our hero to choose for us.

"They'll both have a Cosmo, and I'll have a Dreher. Have them brought to my table." He points across the room to a dark corner away from the dance floor.

"Yes, sir. I'll have them brought right over."

Our knight turns his attention back to us. With a touch of jealousy, I notice his other arm has been around Agnes. He releases both of us, guiding us to stand in front of him. He smiles that dazzling smile I've become so familiar with in recent weeks. His smile would make any woman weak, but that dimple on his right cheek raises the level to universal. He reaches forward and takes our hands in his, instructing us to come with him. He steps between us, striding forward.

Without hesitation, we fall in step behind him. He's like a shepherd parting his flock. Dancers move to either side as he approaches. Agnes looks at me, and I see the same admiration in her eyes. He's in complete control.

As we clear the dance floor, he slows his pace and leans close to us. "Just up these small stairs, that booth in the back."

When we reach the spot, Agnes and I sit together, so close our knees touch. David slides in on the opposite side, positioning himself so he can see the dance floor while also maintaining eye contact.

He extends his hand across the table to Agnes. "You are?"

Agnes takes it. "I'm Agnes, and this is Renata."

He brings her hand to his lips. "Nice to meet you, Agnes."

He releases her hand, extending his hand to me. I fight to keep the smile from parting my lips. He's so natural at this. He looks at me without a flicker of recognition. *What thoughts are lurking behind those dark, magnificent eyes?* I extend my hand to him, feeling his strong, warm hand envelop mine. Like with Agnes, he raises my hand to his lips, kissing it.

"Nice to meet you as well, Renata." He smiles that dazzling smile at both of us. My body still tingles from the feel of his lips on my hand. "I'm sorry for the way that bartender treated you. That's no way to treat a pair of lovely women."

I can't speak, which is fine. Agnes typically does the talking.

"Thank you for helping us," Agnes says.

"I noticed you as soon as you came in. I haven't seen you before. First time?"

He's directing his attention to both of us but primarily Agnes. The table is dark, aside from an artificial candle in the center. His eyes are hooded, but I can see he's taking us both in.

"Yes, our first time." Agnes smiles, turning to me for affirmation. I nod. A woman approaches our table carrying a tray of drinks. She bends down, placing the two cocktails in front of Agnes and me, then reaches across to extend the beer to David. There's recognition in her eyes.

"Thanks, doll," he says, taking the beer.

He watches her walk away before turning back to us. He places his arm on the back of the booth, leaning closer to Agnes. "You were saying?"

"Oh, nothing. I was just saying we haven't been here before."

"I thought so. I would have noticed you." He winks as he says it, taking a drink of his beer. "Try your drinks. Do you like cosmopolitans?"

We don't know. We've never had one. That doesn't stop Agnes. She nods and reaches for hers, but I pull her back. Since we were little girls, Agnes has always worried about fitting into whatever group she finds herself in. She's always cared too much about what others think of her. I've had to watch over her like a mother hen.

Agnes turns and shoots me a withering glance. She reaches again, daring me to stop her. Rather than cause a scene, I let her. She raises the glass to her lips, taking a sip. After a couple more, she sets the drink down, looking back to David, ignoring the disapproving look she's getting from me.

"So, you know our names. Do we get to know yours?"

He smiles. "Oh, I'm sorry. My name is Viktor. But you can call me Vik." He takes another drink of his beer, sliding closer to us.

I fight to hold the surprise from registering on my face. *This wasn't part of the plan. Why has he given her a false name?*

"So, tell me, where are you from? Here in Budapest?"

Agnes shakes her head. "No, we're from a little town in Eastern Hungary. It's called Szerencs. Do you know it?"

"Yeah, over near Miskolc."

Agnes smiles, bobbing her head. "Yep, that's right. I'm surprised. Most Hungarians don't know it unless you live there."

"I have family in Miskolc. I've been out east many times."

For the next fifteen minutes, we talk. David's from Budapest, living in the sixteenth district, not far from us. Unlike us, he grew up here. He tells us he's a regular at the club. That's why everyone knows him. I know Agnes better than I know myself, and I can see she's taken with him. She's finished her drink, and David orders her another. They badger me to try it. I finally relent and take a sip. Agnes's demeanor is changing. Her laughing is more frequent and louder. Even her speech is more boisterous.

David continues to slide closer as we talk. He's right next to Agnes. "So, do you two like to dance?"

Agnes nods, but I hesitate.

David slides out and stands up from the table, extending his hands to us. "Come on. It'll be fun." He's looking at me now, and something inside tells me not to go with him. But I can't say no to his eyes. I relent, longing for my body to be near his. I want to feel his arms around me.

Agnes nearly pushes me out of the seat as David helps me stand. We follow his lead as we make our way onto the dance floor. He walks to the center, making room for us. A few people stop and look in our direction as David pushes through them. He pulls us close. I can feel the warmth of the group pushing against me, the mixture of sweat and perfume. He turns back to us and begins dancing. As we sway to the beat of the music, his attention is on me.

He pulls me close, whispering in my ear, "I hoped you'd come."

I look up at him. "I told you I would."

He stares into my eyes, and his hand slides lower on my back. The music slows, and I rest my head on his chest. I can feel the beat of his heart. *Why had he claimed his name was Vik?* Before I can ask, he steps back, reaching his hand to my cheek. He tips my head around, looking into my eyes. I feel a rush of adrenaline. I've dreamed about this, and now it's happening. His eyes are dark, like the sky at midnight. I can't keep mine open any longer. I long for his lips on mine. I feel him lean into me as his lips press against mine. His kiss is gentle at first. His lips are warm, and I'm overcome with pleasure. I've only known him for a few weeks, but this is the first time I've been close to him. We continue to kiss, becoming more passionate as I feel his tongue against mine.

I'm entirely caught up in his embrace. His strong hands caress my back. I can feel how firm his body is. How fit. After a few more seconds, he pulls his lips from mine, leaning down to whisper in my ear.

"Come on, let's get off the dance floor."

I look into his eyes, unsure. He stares at me with such intensity. I want to go with him. I'm both nervous and excited. And then there's Agnes. I can't leave her. I turn to look for her. She's dancing with two men, one on either side. She loves attention and must be having the time of her life. She'd never forgive me for interrupting. Since we were little girls, she's craved attention from boys. She'll be okay. We won't be gone long.

David takes me by the hand, and I follow him off the dance floor. We walk to the side and head toward a hallway.

Where are we going?

David releases my hand and puts his arm around my shoulders. I nestle in closer, wanting to be with him but feeling unsure. He opens a door, and we're outside. The night is cold, and I regret my outfit. I'm wearing a tiny black dress and a light coat. David pulls me closer, attempting to shield me from the wind. We turn down an alleyway. I hesitate, slowing my step. Something isn't right.

"Where are we going?" I ask.

He doesn't respond, only pulling me closer. In front of us, maybe twenty paces, a man leans against a van smoking a cigarette. The smell of tobacco fills the alley. As we approach, he looks down at his watch, flicking away the butt of the cigarette.

"What took you so long?" he says to David. Not waiting for an answer, his eyes focus on me. I feel his hooded eyes scan me up and down. I've become cattle rather than human.

I try to pull away as my heart races. David has a grip on my shoulders and is much stronger.

The hairy man steps close.

I turn back to David and push my arms against his chest, looking up into his eyes. "What's going on?" I plead. "What are you doing to me?"

David's eyes go soft as he looks at me. His words make my blood run cold.

"I'm sorry, Renata."

At that moment, I know he's not who I think he is. I've been betrayed. I take a big breath, preparing to scream when the large man covers my mouth and picks me up.

Chapter 2

Peter

Perhaps silverback gorillas would make fine Hungarian detectives, Andrassy Peter (in Hungarian surname comes first) thinks as he watches the argument unfolding before him. It's reminiscent of when he visited the New York City Zoo and watched two gorillas fight. This time, there isn't a glass wall separating him from them. Hopefully, this argument won't become as physical as that one did.

Peter sits in the second-floor conference room of the Hungarian National Police headquarters in Budapest. Detective Kovacs Lajos, the head of the human-trafficking task force, disagrees with one of his detectives, Detective Szabo. Each Monday morning, the task force meets to discuss plans for the week. This is Peter's first meeting, and so far, it's done little to impress him. He accepted this job with trepidation, and this display does little to ease his concerns. Peter, a native Hungarian, left Hungary at sixteen for New York City. Now, at fifty-four, he's returned to work as a PI and consultant to the task force.

"What do you think, Peter?"

Peter breaks from his thoughts. Kovacs is speaking to him. Peter notices that all conversation has stopped, and all task force members are staring at him.

"I'm sorry, I was thinking about another aspect of the case. What did you ask me?"

Kovacs frowns and slows his speech. "I said, where do you think they'll move their operation?"

Peter shakes his head. "I don't know. I'm guessing they'll use another restaurant. Maybe a bar? That's where they were before. It would make sense for them to follow the same pattern."

After returning to Hungary following the murder of his wife, Peter began work as a PI. He wanted to focus on lighter cases—theft, infidelity, and insurance fraud. After accepting a simple infidelity case from Kata, his client, he began to follow her husband, Andras. Andras turned out to be much more than an adulterer. He was heavily involved in human trafficking. Peter exposed Andras, causing Andras to try and kill Peter on a train home from Croatia. Andras killed himself in the process, and Peter was asked to join the task force.

Kovacs nods, looking up at the ceiling as he leans back in his chair.

"That's exactly what they're going to do," Detective Szabo, one of the silverback gorillas, nearly yells indignantly. Szabo is a hothead who seems to value his opinion over any others. No doubt, he believes he should be running the task force rather than Kovacs. "We should be putting together a list of restaurants and bars in Budapest. Systematically track them down. That's the only way to find where they've moved their operation."

Kovacs wraps his knuckles on the table, looking sideways at Szabo. "Do you know how many restaurants there are in Budapest? This is a city of two million people. There're hundreds, thousands of bars and restaurants."

Szabo slaps his knee so hard that a clap rings out. "Exactly! Sitting around here talking about it for hours isn't going to help. We need to get to work!"

Peter imagines the two standing up, pounding their chests, and baring their teeth. If not for the inefficiency of it, he might actually like seeing them fight it out. His money would be on Kovacs. Peter knows he needs to be a voice of reason and deescalate the emotion in the room.

"How did they recruit Andras?" Peter asks, and they both turn to look at him.

"What?" Kovacs asks.

"How did Andras get involved in human trafficking? How did they find him?"

Kovacs shrugs. "Good question. I don't know. And I don't think we can ask him, considering you threw him off a train."

Peter glares back at him. "I didn't throw him off a train, he lunged at me, and I dodged it. He was trying to kill me. Remember, he's the one who opened the train doors."

Kovacs nods but has a far-off look in his eye. "You ask an interesting question, Peter; how did the human traffickers recruit him?"

"Who cares how they found him?" Szabo says. "Who cares why he did it? We already know he did, and he's dead. Investigating the past will take too long to impact the present. That's not going to save girls right now."

Kovacs looks back at Szabo and taps his finger on the table. "No... no, Peter's right. If we can figure out how they hired Andras, then we can know where to look. If it worked in the past, it follows they'd try again."

Szabo looks like he's ready to bare his teeth anew. "How are we going to figure that out? Andras is dead. Are you going to go down to Siófok, gather up all his guts, and ask them how he got into trafficking?"

Ignoring Szabo, Peter turns back to Kovacs. "Remember Andras's wife, Kata, the one who hired me? I have a good relationship with her. I also know the bartender from Andras's restaurant. Let me go talk with them. Maybe they can shed some light on how he started."

"Good idea. Why don't you go see what you can learn from them."

Kovacs turns back to Szabo. "Szabo, Varga, and Farkas, start compiling a list of restaurants and bars in Budapest. Let's see how many we're dealing with. We'll give it two days to see which method has more merit."

Chapter 3

Peter

Ten minutes later, Peter sits at his desk in the bullpen of cubicles on the second floor of the police headquarters. This area of the building is set aside for the human-trafficking task force. The desk, made of plain wood, sits nearly empty. A phone rests on one side, a notepad and pen in the middle, and a computer on the other. This is his first time sitting at the desk, and already he's wondering if it should be his last.

"Hey, Peter, can I give you some advice?"

The voice comes from behind, and Peter swivels around in his chair. Szabo stands in front of him, looking down. He's a big man, at least six feet tall and weighing about 230 pounds. He's wearing a shirt and tie and sports a large beer belly. Some of his breakfast remains on the tie hanging from his neck. Peter leans his chair back, craning his neck to look into his eyes. Szabo holds a cup of coffee in his hand.

"You're new here. You just joined the task force. We've all been working on this trafficking syndicate for months. Maybe instead of telling us how we should do our jobs, be a little humbler, and see how it's done first. This isn't America. We do things differently here."

Peter stifles a laugh but can't help the smile that creeps along his face.

"You think this is funny?" Szabo asks.

Peter shakes his head, eying Szabo. "No, not at all. In fact, I think it's about the furthest thing from funny."

Szabo glares down at him. "Well, while you're out investigating a dead man, we'll be in here finding the bad guys. Stopping future abductions. Saving lives. Next time we're in a meeting, maybe shut up and listen, follow our lead, and you might actually learn a thing or two."

Szabo walks to the small table in the middle of the bullpen where Varga and Farkas sit, glaring at Peter. Prior to joining the team, Peter had studied each of their backgrounds. Varga is the youngest member of the team at twenty-four years old. She recently graduated first in her class from a university in Budapest. Farkas isn't much older, in his early thirties. He worked as a uniformed police officer prior to joining the National Police.

Peter hadn't expected a welcome party, but this reception is downright frosty. The entire group seems to be taking exception to a consultant being added, especially since he had lived in the United States longer than in Hungary. But he had anticipated this. Fortunately, he's had plenty of experience with coworkers who haven't liked him. Working with others had never been his strong suit. He never had time for interoffice politics, nor had he ever been willing to bend the rules to appease a coworker.

Swiveling away from them, Peter turns his attention back to his desk. He picks up the badge sitting in the center. It's laminated and includes his picture, complete with the Hungarian National Police seal and the title of "consultant." Not quite the detective badge he had been accustomed to in New York City.

Out of nowhere, a voice sounds from in front of him. "Peter, I'd like to introduce you to Director Toth. He's the head of law enforcement in Hungary."

Kovacs stands at the front of the desk, flanked by another man. Peter stands out of respect. He's the first person Peter has met in the building who's older than himself. He wears a dark suit, white shirt, and dark-blue tie. Both his face and head are clean-shaven. The head is entirely bald, and light shines off it. He has robust features, including a sharply pointed nose and gray eyes. His eyes seem incapable of blinking as they examine Peter. Toth's posture is impeccable as he stands ramrod straight.

"Nice to finally meet you, Peter."

He extends his hand, and Peter grasps it. The hand is meaty and firm.

"Thank you, sir. I appreciate the opportunity."

Toth gives an almost imperceptible nod. "I was grateful for your help on the Dobo Andras case. I'm anxious to see what impact you can make on our task force. Someone of your experience and background should be quite a boon to the team."

"Thank you, sir. I'm not sure how much help I'll be, but I'll do my best."

The director's stare penetrates Peter's soul, and he finds the whole thing unnerving.

"Don't sell yourself short. You have an impressive background. Twenty years with the NYPD, including several promotions and commendations. I expect you'll have valuable insight for us. Do you have everything you need? Kovacs tells me you had a nice idea in the morning meeting. Sounds like you'll be following up on a few leads?"

Peter looks at Kovacs, who's smiling at him. "I know some people who were close to Andras. They might be able to provide us with some insights into how he got into trafficking. Maybe give us some clues on where to look next."

The director's face is impassive, but he gives a nod, never breaking his perfect posture. "Excellent. It'll be nice to gain your perspective on the work. Please let me know if there's anything you need. As you know, Kovacs is running your team, but I'm very anxious to solve this mystery. I stay as involved as I can."

The director walks away, and Peter feels himself relax. He moves to sit back down, but Kovacs remains.

"He's a good boss. He's very supportive of our work here."

Peter nods, and they look at one another. Kovacs shifts his weight from one side to the other. Finally, he makes up his mind, lowering his voice and leaning forward. "Hey, don't let Szabo and the others hold back your ingenuity. I asked the director to add you to the force because of the perspective you can add. You've already started to prove me right with your comments in the meeting this morning."

Kovacs pats him on the shoulder and looks him in the eyes. When he sees Peter has nothing to say, he walks away. Peter sits down, feeling eyeballs boring into him. He glances toward the bullpen finding all three of the other team members watching him. They had witnessed the whole exchange, and their faces illustrate their displeasure. Peter knows this will be a position fraught with danger from both the outside and inside.

Chapter 4

Zsuzsa

"You know, for the longest time, I suspected you were having an affair with him." Kata's looking at me as we stand in the office that has now become hers.

"Me? Why would you think that?"

"Look at you. You're gorgeous. I wish I had the body you have."

This revelation strikes me with confusion. I don't know what to say. I thank her, feeling myself blush. She doesn't realize I'm the one who envies *her*. She's the most elegant woman I've ever known. She moves like she's a dancer in a waltz. She has an unrivaled eye for fashion, and I would kill to have her slender waist and lean muscle tone. I never believed Andras deserved her. He got what he deserved, being cut into a thousand pieces by a speeding train.

"There's something I've always wanted to ask you," she says.

"Ask."

"Did you know?"

"Did I know what? That Andras was having an affair?"

"No, I don't even care about that anymore. Did you know about the trafficking? Did you know he was taking all those young women and sending them to Croatia?"

"Yes and no. Girls would come and work here in the restaurant, then disappear. This business has a lot of turnover, so that wasn't all that unusual. But these girls would vanish. Nobody would ever hear from them again. Something felt wrong."

"What did you do?"

"I asked Andras about it. He passed it off as nothing, but I wouldn't let it go. I kept pressing." I can still feel goosebumps as I think about that day. "He grabbed me by the arm, squeezing hard. He told me to keep my mouth shut and stop asking questions. Then he threatened me. He told me if I told anyone else, I'd disappear too."

Kata stands from her desk and comes around to me. She gives me a hug. I can feel my body shaking, remembering that day.

"I'm so sorry, Zsuzsa. I had no idea. How long ago was that?"

"Only a couple of months. Then you hired Peter, and he exposed the whole thing. Andras was killed, and I can sleep safe and sound again. I guess both of us can."

Kata stands with her arm on my shoulder, holding my hand. "Do you ever wonder where they've gone?"

"Who? The girls?"

"Yes, them. But the traffickers. Andras was working for someone. They haven't been caught. Girls are probably still disappearing somewhere."

I sense the presence of someone else. Margit, the cook, stands at the door of the office. She gives us a curious look. I'm sure we look odd, standing in the office holding each other.

"Sorry to interrupt, Zsuzsa, your food is up."

"Go," Kata tells me. "We can talk later."

I head out of the office following Margit. My life has changed dramatically since Andras was killed two weeks ago on the train returning to Budapest. I no longer live in fear for my life. It's hard to express the emotional toll that takes on a person. I was wound up so tight I felt like a spring stretched too far.

The difference between Kata and Andras is remarkable. Now I feel like I work for someone who cares about me. She's the sweetest and kindest person. It's a joy for me to come to work. She's amazing. She's the widow, she lost her husband and found out all these horrible things about him, yet she's comforting me. I don't think I could do that if I were in her shoes.

I enter the bar and step back into the kitchen as Margit hands me the food.

"Sorry to interrupt, but it was getting cold."

I tell her I'm glad she did and walk back out. I place the food in front of my customer.

"Stuffed Peppers, just like your momma used to make," I tell him.

I notice Agoston is done with his food, and I clear his plate bringing him the bill. Agoston has been coming to Szép Ilona's ever since I left working for him in the club and moved over here. He picks it up and looks at it, then drops plenty of forint on the counter to cover the cost and leave me a nice tip. I reach to pick it up, and he grabs my hand.

"Zsuzsa, what can I do to get you to come work at Club Ötkert?"

I look into his eyes. Every time he comes, he tries. And every time I turn him down. I don't want to go back to working in a club. Not because of him. I like him. I don't want the club environment anymore. That's for women much younger than me. I might have been willing before, with Andras, but not now. I won't leave Kata.

"Nothing. I don't want to go back, and you know that."

"How about just part-time? Just on the weekends. I'm sure you could use the extra money. I need someone with your experience."

I chuckle. "Is that your way of telling me I've gotten old and you want to work with someone more mature than the kids you have there?"

He shakes his head and flashes a crooked smile. "You aren't old yet." He furrows his eyebrows. "But seriously, I need someone like you. Someone who won't make a mountain of every molehill that comes along."

I shake my head. "I'll let you know if I ever change my mind. But I love being here now and don't want anything else."

He shrugs, puts on his coat, and heads out the door telling me he'll see me again soon.

As I return to work, serving my customers food and drink, I can't stop thinking about what Kata asked me. Where have the traffickers gone? Where are they operating now? I hope I never find out.

Chapter 5

Peter

Peter looks through the big glass doors of the Hungarian National Police Headquarters. He needs fresh air. The big building is already starting to suffocate him. It's been a couple of years since he has worked in an office, and he's unsure if he can do it again. Maybe a walk outside will clear his head. It's December in Budapest, and although cold, the sun is shining.

As he pushes through the outside doors, he feels the thud of another body smashing into his. This shape is small and feminine, and he feels remorse as the head of long, dark hair snaps backward, and the woman falls to the ground.

"I'm sorry," Peter exclaims and bends to help her.

As he extends toward her, he's taken aback by the tears streaming down her face. Her eyes are red and swollen, and she looks like she's been crying for hours.

"What's wrong?" he asks, helping her to her feet.

The girl looks at him, trying to talk, but all that comes out is a gut-wrenching sob.

"Let me help you," Peter says.

He takes her arm and guides her to a park bench outside the building. The girl keeps her head down, allowing him to lead her. As they sit, she puts her head in her hands and continues to sob. Peter isn't sure what to do. He can't help wondering what's going on.

After several minutes of body-shaking cries, she seems to get a hold of her emotions. Her dark hair covers her face as she leans over, obstructing Peter's view. She wipes at her face with the palm of her hands, trying to clear the tears from her eyes.

"Are you a policeman?" she asks.

He is, and he isn't. But he sees little point in confusing the girl right now. "Yes, I am."

She's still leaning over. Peter can't see her face, but her head bobs up and down.

"I need your help. My friend was taken." Her body erupts into sobs again. She looks up, tears streaming down her face. Her eyes are swollen. "It's my fault she's gone."

Peter puts a hand on her back, and he can feel her shaking. "I'd be happy to help. What do you mean she was taken? Who took her?"

The girl again fights for control over her emotions. Soon, the sobs and shaking slow. She straightens, and Peter removes his hand from her back.

She brushes back her hair and wipes her eyes. "I don't know who took her. We were at a club. She was dancing with a guy, and I was dancing with some other guys. We got separated, and then I couldn't find her. I looked everywhere."

Peter nods. "Could she have gone home with the guy? Maybe nobody took her."

The girl shakes her head, putting a hand on Peter's knee. "No! She would never do that. She didn't even want to go to the club. I'm the one who convinced her. She's shy. She's never been with a boy."

Peter feels his pulse quicken as he considers the implications of her words. He leans closer to the girl. "Come inside. We need to find your friend."

Chapter 6

Peter

Peter ushers the girl up the stairs, through the large bullpen area, and into the small conference room, winning looks from several people. No doubt her red eyes and wet cheeks raised questions. After entering the room, he pulls out a seat and helps her sit at the head of the small four-person table. He sits across from her and pushes a box of tissues toward her.

She's no longer crying. She sits holding the tissue to her nose and dabbing at her eyes. He needs to be careful. Her emotions are raw, and he doesn't want to set her off again.

Peter's conflicted watching her. Kovacs should hear this; and having another set of ears would be good. Two perspectives are almost always better than one. Countless times in his past, as a cop and detective, his partner had caught something he had missed. But would he lose the girl? Would she feel overwhelmed by two older men interviewing her? Would she become a turtle and hide in her shell? Kovacs could be intimidating, and Peter had built a rapport with her.

A soft knock sounds at the door, and they turn to see Kovacs in the door frame. He motions to Peter with his index finger, bidding him to come out, and closes the door.

Peter stands. "Can I get you anything? Coffee? Tea?" he says to the girl.

She shakes her head, then stops. "Actually, can I have some water?"

"Be right back."

As Peter exits, Kovacs stands in the bullpen area, leaning against a desk. "Who is she?"

Peter shrugs. "That's what I'm trying to find out. She nearly ran me over outside. Her roommate is gone, and she thinks someone has taken her."

Kovacs raises an eyebrow but says nothing. That patience, that "nothing" makes up Peter's mind.

"Will you come in with me to talk with her?"

"I'd be happy to."

Peter turns to walk back into the small conference room but stops. "She asked for some water. But I don't know where our break room is."

Kovacs smiles. "Sorry, I should have shown you. I keep forgetting this is your first day."

He points down the hall, and Peter sees the kitchen area.

When Peter returns, he finds Kovacs still waiting for him outside the room. He hasn't gone in. Peter acknowledges the wisdom of asking Kovacs to join him. Kovacs is head of the task force; he can do whatever he likes. But instead, he waited for Peter.

The girl is pacing back and forth by the window. As they enter, she looks in their direction, stops, and tugs on her lower lip, eyeing Kovacs.

"This is Detective Kovacs," Peter explains, motioning to him. "Would it be all right if he joins us while we talk? He's my partner and can help."

She says nothing continuing to pull on her lower lip. Finally, she shrugs and sits back down. Peter places a bottle of water on the table in front of her, taking his seat. Kovacs pulls out the chair across from the girl, the furthest seat from her. He's yet to say anything, allowing Peter to lead.

The girl grabs the water bottle, opens it, and brings it to her lips, tossing back her head. She takes several large gulps, drinking most of it before bringing it back down. She replaces the lid but doesn't put it back on the table. Instead, she clutches it to her chest. Almost like a security blanket. She looks at both of them, then looks away.

"Is it okay if we ask you a few questions? Our top priority is to help you find your friend, but we'll need some information to do that. Does that make sense?"

The girl nods, only looking at Peter. She continues to clutch the water bottle to her body.

Kovacs takes out a tape recorder and places it on the table. The girl sees it and shoots a look at Peter.

"It would help us if we could record our conversation, make sure we don't miss anything. Is that okay?" Peter explains.

The girl leans away, almost like it's a snake that might bite, but she nods.

Peter knows he needs to turn her attention and get her to relax.

"Great. Let's start with a few simple questions. What's your name, and where are you from?"

"My name is Kiss Agnes. I'm from Eastern Hungary, a town called Szerencs."

She looks down, preferring not to make eye contact.

"What's your friend's name? The one that went missing?"

She looks up at Peter, "Németh Renata."

"And how do you know Renata?"

Tears spring to her eyes. "She's been my best friend as long as I can remember. We grew up together in Szerencs."

Peter nods. He's keeping the questions simple. "I can see why this is so hard for you. We're going to do everything we can to get her back. Can you tell me what happened? When did she go missing?"

Agnes drops her head and holds the water bottle in her lap. She plays with the label wrapped around it.

"We went to a club last night, Club Ötkert. Have you heard of it?"

She looks up, eyeing Peter, but when he shakes his head, she turns to Kovacs. Kovacs nods but says nothing.

"We got separated when we were dancing in the club, and when I looked for her, I couldn't find her. I thought maybe she went back home to our apartment, but when I got there, she wasn't there either. That's when I knew something had happened to her."

"How did you get separated?" Peter asks.

"Well, we went onto the dance floor with Vik. We were all dancing together. Then a couple of guys started dancing with me, and Vik and Renata danced together. When I turned around, they were gone."

Peter and Kovacs exchange a look.

Peter asks, "Who's Vik?"

Agnes shakes her head. "He was this nice guy we met at the club. He got us a couple drinks. Before we started dancing, we sat and talked with him for a while."

"Had you ever seen Vik before? Did either of you know him?"

"No, we didn't know him. He helped us out with the bartender, who was a jerk. I think he liked Renata, though. He couldn't stop staring at her. But that's nothing new."

"What do you mean?"

Agnes looks at him with exasperation. "She's gorgeous. All the boys like her. They always have."

Peter nods, making a note on his notepad.

"How long had you been dancing with these other men? How long until you noticed Vik and Renata were gone?"

Agnes looks up to the ceiling, calculating the time. "I don't know. We got to the club around ten, and I got home around midnight. We talked with Vik for about twenty minutes. Maybe an hour altogether. No more than an hour and a half."

Agnes looks back at them, placing the water bottle on the table. She's making eye contact now.

"So maybe Renata isn't missing. Maybe she's—"

"No," Agnes stresses, "she'd never go home with a guy."

"Why are you so sure?"

She places her hand on the table and leans forward. "Because Renata never has. She's a virgin. She's never had sex. She's too shy."

Peter leans back in his chair, rubbing his beard. "Is there any particular reason you picked Club Ötkert?"

"What do you mean?"

"Why that club?"

"Renata kinda suggested it."

"What do you mean *kinda*?" Peter asks.

Agnes shrugs. "Yesterday morning, we talked before we went to work. Since we had come up to Budapest, we hadn't done anything fun, and I was complaining about it. I tried to get Renata to go to a club with me, but she never would. She's shy. Anyway, we talked, and I told her I wanted to go out. She suggested Club Ötkert."

"How did she know about the club?"

"I don't know. I was so excited that I didn't care. We both went to work, and when we got home, we got ready and went to the club."

"You work together?" Peter asks.

"No, I work as a server in a small restaurant. She's a barista in a coffee shop."

"What brought you to Budapest?"

"I always wanted to move up here. After school, I convinced Renata that we should."

"When was that?"

"Five months ago."

Peter makes a note on his notepad.

"How old are you?"

She looks young, and Peter has been wondering about this since she ran into him.

"Seventeen."

"Renata too?"

Agnes nods.

For the first time, Kovacs speaks. "Agnes, we'll need to contact your family and Renata's."

"No!" Agnes stands from the table.

Peter stands too, extending his hands. "Okay... okay. We won't do anything without telling you first. Let's just sit back down."

Agnes shakes her head and bites her lip, but instead of sitting back down, she turns and walks to the window. Looking out over Budapest, she shakes her head again. "Our families don't know where we are. We didn't exactly leave with their blessing."

Chapter 7

Peter

"No! We don't even know if the girl is truly missing." Detective Kovacs is standing at the head of the table, glaring at the rest of the task force.

Like in the previous meeting, Detective Szabo thinks his opinion is the only one that matters. The power tug-of-war is in full effect.

"We aren't just going to go into that club and start asking questions. If we do, we might lose the opportunity to find who's in charge. Someone is orchestrating the whole thing. We have two objectives here. First, find Renata. Second, find who's taking these girls. If we do it right, we can accomplish both."

Szabo shoots an icy glare at Kovacs but says nothing. For once, he seems to sense it's time to shut up. He's been arguing that they need to infiltrate the club. Guns blazing. Stop wasting time. As usual, Varga and Farkas seem to be with him.

Kovacs paces.

As Peter watches him, his own mind works. Are they really so sure the girl is missing? She's seventeen and met an older man at the club. Agnes is convinced she wouldn't go home with the man, but Peter isn't. Plenty of seventeen-year-old girls go home with men they don't know. This could be a whole lot to do about nothing. She could turn up at home anytime in the next couple of days, unaware she had been considered missing.

On the other hand, something sinister could have happened to her. But that doesn't mean it's trafficking related. Could it be an isolated incident? Maybe the guy raped her. Perhaps he raped her and killed her. Who even is "the guy?" Maybe it's trafficking but unrelated to the group that had hired Andras.

"Peter, what are you thinking?" Kovacs asks.

Peter hadn't noticed that Kovacs was no longer pacing. He and the rest of the group are watching him. Szabo forces out an elongated breath turning away.

"Well," Peter begins, "I was thinking we really have no idea what happened or if anything ever did happen. And until we do, any reaction would be a mistake."

Szabo is leaning back in his chair, looking out the window of the conference room. He spins to face Peter, his voice rising in anger.

"So you just want to leave this girl on her own? She could be alive right now, and immediate action on our part might save her life."

Peter doesn't talk to Szabo when he responds. He speaks to Kovacs. "Yes, she could be alive and in trouble. But even if that's true, we don't know if this Vik regularly went to that club. Agnes's description sounds like he did, but we don't know that for sure. And if we ask a bunch of questions, we lose the element of surprise. Nobody in the club knows we have any suspicions about it."

Kovacs bobs his head, looking up at the ceiling. "We need a plant. Maybe more than one. We get a couple of girls who look like Renata and put them in the club. See if this Vik will take the bait."

"I'll do it," Varga says.

They all turn and look in her direction.

"I'm not seventeen, but maybe I don't have to be. Maybe not every girl they take is that young."

"That's true," Peter says. "Nobody would know you there. We know Andras would prey on foreign women, or women new to Budapest. This group probably does the same. Fewer people to miss them."

Kovacs sits down at the table and leans back in his chair. "I like it. We could give you a cover story. You could be alone, desperate."

Varga smiles. "Sounds like fun."

Chapter 8
Detective Kovacs

I sit in my car, listening for the school bell, replaying the interview with Agnes in my mind. It's not what she said but how Peter handled it that I can't let go. I'm not new to interrogations or witness interviews. I've conducted a countless number. But women, especially young women, have never been my forte. For at least the second time in the day, I'm grateful to have Peter on the force. He didn't simply ask questions; he led her. She was emotional, and he calmed her. He drew out observations she didn't even know she had made. His ability to read and interpret body language made me jealous. Could this be a result of the difference in our training? I was brought up in a communist regime. My training was about suppressing and intimidating people. Being trained and having a career in America, Peter has a different approach. I can learn so much from him.

At first, I thought we were dealing with a random abduction. Maybe not even a kidnapping. A young girl goes home with an older man. The same scenario probably happened in that same club that night. But that wasn't enough for Peter. Agnes was convinced she had been taken, and he trusted her judgment, or at least gave her opinion the benefit of the doubt. He was humble. His questions were specific. He asked about their body language.

When questions began to highlight inconsistencies, Peter expertly drilled deeper. He kept the conversation light and never let the girl feel like she was being interviewed. Instead, she felt in control. Like she was guiding the conversation, sharing everything she knew. As the interview progressed, we both felt the same. Renata knew Vik. The challenge now was to find out who Vik was. How he knew Renata. And why Renata didn't tell Agnes.

The buzz of the bell pulls me from my thoughts, and I open my car door. I stayed in the car while waiting, which isn't normal. Typically, I'll get out and have a cigarette. I won't smoke in the car. Noemi hates the smell of cigarettes, and I worry about the effects of secondhand smoke. Just because I don't value my health doesn't mean I don't care about my daughter's.

Bundled kids stream out of the front doors. What is it about kids and the idea of a bit of freedom? You'd almost think someone offered a million forint to the first one hundred out the door. I was the same way when I was a kid. I never liked school, especially all the rules. Is that why I went into law enforcement? I can make the rules rather than have them dictated to me.

Nearing the front doors, I see the gleam of my daughter's chair reflecting the last remaining sun. Noemi has her bag on her lap, keeping her arms free to push the wheels of her chair. A classmate, Ildiko, holds the door. What a sweet girl she is.

As I approach, Noemi makes eye contact, and we share our trademark wink. I don't even remember where it started.

"How are you, beautiful?" I ask, leaning down to kiss both cheeks.

She forces a smile, not making eye contact. "I'm okay."

I study her face, but she doesn't seem to want to say more, or at least not here. I turn to Ildiko, "Thank you for helping her. Can I offer you a ride home?"

She shakes her head. "No, thank you, Mr. Kovacs. I have to help our teacher with something. My mom is going to come to get me later."

I nod and step behind Noemi, pushing her chair toward the car. Ildiko calls out a goodbye, and Noemi waves.

When we reach the car, I open the rear passenger door and lift her in, fastening the seat belt. I open the trunk and collapse her chair, placing it inside. After getting behind the wheel and starting the car, I glance at her in the rearview mirror. Usually, sensing her mood, I'd ask what's wrong. But I stop, thinking of Peter and how he had handled Agnes today.

"You sure look pretty."

She just stares out the window. "Some people don't think so."

I pull onto the road and lean to the side to see her better in the mirror. "Only blind people."

She doesn't react, opting to stare out the window. My natural inclination is to ask who "some people" are, but I force myself to be patient.

We drive for five minutes in silence when she finally speaks again.

"Why are boys so stupid?"

I look at her in the rearview mirror. She looks at the back of my head, her eyes searching.

"Well, I'm really not supposed to tell you this. But boys have brains the size of ping-pong balls. Considering that... I think we do pretty well."

She fights it, she doesn't want to, but finally she smiles. "Dad... I'm serious."

"So am I. At least we've evolved. Two hundred years ago, our brains were the size of almonds."

I hold up my hand, giving her a visualization. My favorite sound in the world erupts from her. She giggles.

"Did a boy do something stupid today?"

She looks back out the window. The smile vanishes. "Miklos."

"What did Miklos do?"

"He said I couldn't be on their team because I would slow them down. He said I was a baby."

I fight the urge to demand Miklos's last name, return to school, and arrest him. But I know better. Arresting a ten-year-old would be frowned upon. It might even get me on the eleven o'clock news.

"I had a Miklos today in my work also."

"You did?"

"Well, I do almost every day. The Miklos at work thinks he should be the leader, not me. Sometimes he's not very nice."

"So what did you do?"

"I considered punching him in the face." I chuckle. "But then I thought of you and your mom and decided to ignore him. I reminded myself I was chosen to be the leader, not him."

I can see my words sinking in.

"You know how to get Miklos back?"

"How?"

"You do the very best in everything you can. You study hard, and you try your best. You show him and everyone else that it's their loss if they don't have you on their team."

She frowns. "He's right, though."

"How is he right?"

"I can't walk. I'm not a good teammate."

We reach the house, and I put the car in park. I turn around and look at her.

"Do you remember what I said about boys having ping-pong brains?"

She gives me an exasperated look.

"You have a brain the size of a watermelon. In fact, you must have the strongest neck in the world to keep your head from falling over. When I was your age, I had a friend who was blind. He couldn't see a thing. I'd always try and sneak up on him to scare him, but he always knew I was there. How do you think he knew?"

"He smelled you." She gave me a teasing smile, which made me laugh.

"Almost right. He heard me. Even when I tried to be completely silent, he heard me. You might never be a great football or basketball player, but there are other things that people like Miklos will never be able to compete with you in. You just keep developing your brain. Don't worry too much about what you can't do. Work on making yourself better in what you can do."

She smiles, and I know she's feeling better.

"Now, let's get inside and see if your mom has anything for dinner."

Chapter 9

Agnes

Why did I come to Budapest? Renata would be okay if I weren't so stupid and stubborn. She'd still be alive. Maybe my mother's right. I am selfish.

I look up, realizing we've come to my stop. The bus is jammed with people, making an exit difficult. My stop is close to the police headquarters, but at Deák Ferenc Square, a mass of people entered, pushing me to the back. Now I fight my way past them, apologizing as I climb.

"I need to get off," I call out, squeezing up the aisle of standing passengers.

One man with a big belly leans his head back and sighs in exasperation. Several passengers, having nowhere else to go, exit the bus. Eventually, everyone in the aisle either exits or moves enough for me to get by.

Stepping off the bus, I try to ignore the angry faces of the passengers waiting to reboard. It's not my fault. Why is it that everything I do seems to be wrong? Or at least I'm blamed for it. The air has turned cold, and I quicken my pace. The bus was stifling with its limited airflow and mass of humanity. That's been one part of Budapest I've not liked. I hate being close to strangers. Growing up in a little village in the country made me claustrophobic in large crowds.

The walk to my apartment is only a few minutes from the bus stop, and I cover the distance quickly. Maybe Renata will be in the apartment when I get there. Maybe she wasn't taken. The detectives could be right. She might have stayed with Vik. I might not know her as well as I think. But even as I think it, I don't believe it. Renata couldn't even look at a boy, let alone talk to one. I can't even remember a time when she did. The boys always tried to talk to her. They liked her. She's pretty. But she couldn't talk back, even to the ones she liked. She'd hide and giggle, then find an excuse to leave. Eventually, they'd give up. She hated it but couldn't stop it from happening.

I see shadows expanding across the street as I reach our apartment building. The sun hasn't disappeared, but it's getting dark. Below-freezing temperatures are typical, but we haven't seen the first snowstorm yet. Renata and I share an apartment on the third floor of a six-floor building in the tenth district, called Kőbánya. The building is a lakótelep, a big square slab of cement constructed by the communists during the Cold War. In Hungary, like many other Eastern Bloc countries, the communists stole the private citizens' farms. They moved them into the city to work in factories. Their homes and farms became the property of the state. The workforce moved to the cities and occupied the thousands of lakóteleps.

As I reach the third floor, my floor, I anxiously fumble with my keys. Even though I know Renata isn't inside, I can't help hoping. I open the door and look in, and my spirit sinks. Everything is just as I'd left it. Renata is nowhere to be found. I feel the tears begin again as I walk to the bedroom. I'm exhausted, having barely slept last night and spending the day at the police station. I want a bed, but I don't go to my own. I lay down on Renata's, pulling her blanket around me.

I feel desperately alone as I lay there staring up at the ceiling, breathing her scent. She and I have always been together. We left home and came to Budapest only a few months ago. Renata has always been my support. We've been inseparable since we were six years old. What am I going to do without her? I can't afford this apartment on my own. We could barely pay for it together. I long for my mother. No, not my mother. She finds fault in everything I do. Instead, I wish for the mother I should have had. The type of mother who supports her daughter. The type who encourages, not mandates. The kind I could go to with fears. Tears begin to fall onto Renata's pillow, and I can't believe I have any left. I've cried all day.

The silence is interrupted by a buzzing noise, then a knock on the front door. I jump up, wiping at my eyes. *Maybe it's Renata?* No. She has her own keys. But she could have lost them. Or it could be the police. Maybe they found her. My hopes soar as I reach the door, throwing it open. I don't recognize the face staring back at me. It's a man in his early twenties. He's muscular, with dark hair and bright-green eyes. A gold chain dangles from his neck, visible through his unzipped black leather jacket.

"Yes, can I help you?"

He doesn't answer right away. Instead, he looks down at a piece of paper, then back up at me. His eyes are penetrating. I feel drawn to him.

"Are you Agnes?"

"Yes."

"Renata sent me. She wanted me to come and get you."

At the mention of her name, my hope soars.

"You know where she is? Where is she?"

"Not far. Come on. I'll take you to her."

I invite him in, telling him I need to grab a few things before we go. I can't believe it. She's okay! She's close by. I feel like a thousand pounds have been lifted from my shoulders. I walk back into the bedroom and grab my jacket and purse.

As I return to the door, I notice he's looking around the apartment. It's not curiosity. He's looking for something. His behavior makes me pause, and I slow my step. *Am I being too trusting?*

"So, how do you know Renata?" I keep my voice light, as if I'm merely curious, making conversation. But I'm watching his eyes, analyzing him.

He hesitates. "Uh... I really don't know her well. She's with a friend of mine."

I smile. "Who's your friend?" I relax a little. He's a friend of Vik.

"David." He's still looking around the apartment, barely paying attention to me.

I freeze as I begin to turn the handle of the exterior door. He notices my reaction, and I see him stiffen. I turn to look at him. *He doesn't know Renata. Who is he?*

"You know, maybe I should use the toilet before I go."

I release the door handle and walk back down the hall. As I pass him, he reaches out and grabs my wrist. His grip is hard. His hand feels like a vice, and I gasp in pain.

"You can use the toilet when we get there," he says, pulling me toward the door.

He's much more powerful than me. The pull is effortless, and my body is dragged toward him. I try to pull away when I see his other hand come up. I try to duck, but he's too fast. He slaps at my head, hitting me around the ear. The blow is hard, and I see stars. My eyes go dark momentarily, and he grabs my other wrist. He's holding both wrists and pulls me to him. His breath wreaks of tobacco. I fight the vomit rising in my stomach as he whispers, "That was a warning. If you struggle any more, I'll kill you and Renata." He smiles.

My next movement is instinctive. I look him in the eye and spit into it. He releases one of my wrists to wipe his face, and I yank out an arm and hit him with my free hand. He releases me in surprise, and I dart toward the kitchen. He screams obscenities, stalking my way. I need something to defend myself, but what? A knife!

I'd left a cutting knife in the sink yesterday. I scramble that way, but he grabs my hair just before I reach it. He pulls hard, and I cry out. My head rocks back, and I turn and swing my right hand. I connect with the side of his face, freeing myself from his grasp. I can feel burning at the back of my head. I reach the sink and frantically plunge my hand into the soapy water. He reaches for me, as I feel the handle of the knife. I grasp it tight in my palm, whipping back toward him, swinging it wildly. I had hoped to strike him near his heart, but instead, I slash his gut. He screams out in agony. He reaches his hand to his stomach and looks down. As he raises his hand to his face, bright crimson stains his fingers and palm. His face is white as he stumbles backward. I grip the knife tighter, stepping toward him. He continues to stumble, looking at me and the knife.

Then he turns his back to me, stumbling around the corner toward the apartment door. I can't feel any pain; the blood is coursing through my body with adrenaline. My grip on the knife is so tight my knuckles are white. I hear him at the door, swinging it open. I sneak around the corner, but he's gone. Big drops of blood cover the hallway. I look at the door—a bloody handprint is all that remains.

Chapter 10

Peter

Peter arrives at the apartment building and is greeted by two uniformed police officers while making his way to the front door.

"Who are you?" the younger one asks. He's tall and sports a mustache. He looks like his idol might be Tom Selleck in *Magnum, PI*. They stand in front of him, blocking his entrance.

Peter reaches inside his jacket and pulls out the laminated card identifying him.

"What's this?" the older one asks, taking it from him.

"I'm a consultant with the National Police."

The man looks up from the badge studying Peter's face, shrugs, and waves him in. The elevator in the lobby is blocked off with caution tape. Standing by the stairs is a blonde woman in a long black leather jacket, navy-blue skirt, and heels.

"Who are you?" she asks.

"Andrassy Peter. I work as a consultant for the human-trafficking task force of the National Police."

He holds out his credential, and she takes it from him, scrutinizing it. After examining it, she hands it back.

"What are you doing here?"

"The girl who was attacked was in our offices today. She called me afterward. We're investigating the disappearance of her friend, Renata."

The woman eyes him skeptically. "The girl is up on the third floor. She needs to go to the hospital for an evaluation. You can go up to see her, but don't touch anything. Forensics is still gathering evidence. And be careful where you step. There's blood on the stairs."

Peter nods, promising to be careful.

As he reaches the third floor, he finds Agnes sitting on a chair. He's surprised to see she's not crying. She's staring down at the floor as if in a trance. Not wanting to startle her, he approaches slowly and speaks softly.

"Agnes? It's me, Peter."

His voice brings her out of her thoughts, and she looks up, showing no sign of recognition. Realization suddenly strikes, and she exclaims, "Oh, Peter!" She rises from her chair, throwing her arms around him. He's surprised. She's sobbing, her body trembling.

After several seconds, she gains control of the crying, releases him, and steps back. Her eyes are red and swollen. Her exhaustion is palpable. He doesn't want to, but he knows he needs to ask her a few questions. He puts his hands on her shoulders and makes eye contact with her.

"Agnes, who attacked you? Did you know the man?"

She shakes her head.

"What was he looking for?"

Agnes tells him the man claimed to know Renata. He promised to take her to her. She had known he was lying when he said the man's name was David rather than Vik.

Aside from asking a couple of clarifying questions about the knife, Peter listens without speaking. His eyebrows rise after hearing she cut his abdomen. When he's satisfied she's told him everything, he escorts her down to the female officer at the bottom of the stairs.

"Agnes, they want to take you to be evaluated at the hospital. Do you mind if I look around your apartment?"

She's shaking, and he holds her by the elbow, indicating to the female officer that she should take her now.

"No, I don't mind," Agnes says. She starts to walk away, then turns back to him. "Peter? Am I going to be safe?"

Peter looks at the female officer, and she nods.

"This officer will take you to the hospital to be evaluated. We'll make sure to always have someone with you."

The female officer approaches and wraps a blanket around Agnes's shoulders. She holds Agnes under her arm as they walk out. Peter watches them go, then heads to the apartment, thinking about what she'd told him. This man coming to attack Agnes proves they're dealing with something serious. Renata has been abducted. That's no longer in doubt. She's also likely still alive but in serious trouble.

What was the man looking for? Agnes said he had a note with her name. He had clearly come to get her, but why? If they wanted her, why didn't they take her that night in the club? What has changed since then?

He reaches the apartment but finds it's still being investigated by forensics. Rather than disturb them, he waits outside. The good news is that the abductor went no further than the kitchen. They don't need to investigate the entire apartment. After only a few minutes, they finish and tell him he can enter. He starts in the kitchen, making sure nothing is out of place. Everything he sees corroborates Agnes's story. Next, he examines the bathroom. Nothing unusual there. Finally, he enters the bedroom. The decor is simple, like any teenage girl's room. A poster of an American boy band, NSYNC, hangs on one wall. On the other, a collage of pictures. Renata and Agnes, along with family members, friends, and pets, are featured in the collage. A vase of flowers adorns the top of one dresser, but the other is plain. Peter doesn't want to snoop or invade the girl's privacy, but he needs to be thorough.

Neither dresser contains anything of genuine interest, and he's about to give up when he reaches under the mattress of one of the beds. He feels something hard. Pulling it out, he finds a book adorned with gold lettering and a lock. Easily picking the lock, he opens the book. A photo is glued to the first page. Although quite a bit younger, Peter recognizes Renata. He turns the page finding the first entry, dated March 27, 1996:

Dear Diary, I think that's how you do it. This is my first entry. Today was my birthday. Aunt Agi got this diary for me. What should I write? I went to school, and everyone sang to me. Agnes gave me a stuffed monkey. Dominick gave me a card wishing me a happy birthday. He drew a picture of a flower on it. He came over and handed it to me after school. I was so shy I couldn't say anything but thanks. I could tell he wanted to say something, but he didn't. When I got home, Mom made me my favorite, paprikás krumpli and chocolate cake. I'm going to write in here every day.

The following entry is dated April 24, 1996. So much for writing every day. The entry is simple, she had done well on a test, and Dominick smiled at her when walking home with Renata. Peter turns the pages, skimming the entries, unsure what he's looking for. The entries are sporadic and often weeks or months apart. He finally stops on an entry dated December 9, 2000—only four days ago:

Today was a pretty good day, other than Mr. Varga. I don't know what his problem is. He's always so rude. He thinks of me more as a slave than an employee. It's so annoying. I hate him! I can't wait to get back to school and out of this job.

But it's not all bad. I get to see some nice men every once in a while, even if it's just for a few seconds here and there. David was in the shop again today. He's so handsome. I can feel my heart flutter every time he walks in. At first, he would only come once or twice a week, but now he seems to be coming every morning.

I wish I could say more, but I'm too shy. I don't know how people do it. I love it when he comes in, but I can't wait for him to leave. He stayed longer today. He asked where I was from and what brought me to Budapest. He asked me if I had a boyfriend. Eeek! I couldn't help smiling then. He was looking down at me with those beautiful eyes. When I told him no, he asked me to come to a club with him on Friday. When I told him I couldn't because I was going to be with Agnes, he told me to bring her. I told him I would think about it.

What would Agnes say about me liking an older man? I could never tell her.

Peter looks up from the diary and makes eye contact with Justin Timberlake, who's staring down at him from the poster. David was the same name used by the abductor when he replied to Agnes. Peter turns the page to the final entry. Friday, December 1, 2000:

David was in the shop again today. He's so sweet. I told him I would go to the club tonight but made him promise that he wouldn't show Agnes that we know each other. I don't want her to know about him until she meets him. I want to see what she thinks of him. He promised that he'd make it seem like we had never met. I asked Agnes if she wanted to go to a club tonight, and she was so excited. I guess we're going. I'm excited but so nervous. I don't know if I'll really go.

Peter closes the book. Things just got a lot more interesting.

Chapter 11

Renata

"Renata? Will you help your sister?"

I look at my reflection in the mirror. Why can't Mom ever give me a break? It's always Renata, do this, Renata, do that. Usually, whatever she needs revolves around Anna. My little sister is so helpless. Turning back to the mirror, I begin brushing my hair. Today is the last day of gymnasium (the Hungarian equivalent to high school). To celebrate, the school is holding a dance. *Maybe Dominick will ask me to dance.* The thought makes me smile. I imagine how I might react if he asks me. I practice my smile in the mirror.

My smile morphs into a frown as I look down at my dress. It's the only dress I have, and although I've saved it for special occasions, it shows signs of wear. The trim is beginning to fray, and there's a spot where the fabric is wearing thin. The dress was a gift from my parents on my fourteenth birthday. Little did I know at the time it would be the last gift I would ever receive from my father. Looking back in the mirror, I imagine a new dress. Something less girl and more woman, a dress boys might consider sexy. Maybe tight and red with matching heels. Something that might draw attention and make the other girls jealous.

"Renata! Stop looking at yourself in the mirror and help your sister!"

Mom storms into the bedroom Anna and I share. Anna is twelve years old, five years younger than me. As usual, she's almost helpless. She was born with a deformity in her right arm. After just a couple days of life, the arm became infected, and doctors had to amputate it.

"It's okay, Mom. I can manage."

Anna is struggling to pull her dress on.

Mom glares at me, pointing at Anna. "Renata, help her!" She turns back and heads toward the kitchen.

I glare at Anna, but watching her struggle makes me feel remorse. Her dress is on now, but she can't button the back.

I tell her, "Anna, you should have gotten up earlier." I go to her, helping her button the back of her dress and buckle her shoes. Nudging her over to the mirror, I begin brushing her hair.

Anna senses the change in me. She looks hopeful as she stares at my reflection in the mirror. "Do you think Dominick will dance with you today?"

I frown. Her comment cuts at my soul. I have been worrying about this since I woke up. Dominick has been my school crush for nine years. The whole family knows how much I care for him, even if I won't admit it.

"Probably not. Who do you want to dance with?"

Anna's face falls. "Nobody wants to dance with the one-armed girl."

My heart aches for her. Although Anna will be striking in a few years, she's probably right that boys won't pay attention to her because of her disability. A surge of love swells in me, and I lean over, kissing her cheek. "If those boys don't dance with you, it's their loss, not yours."

"Girls! Get in here and eat! You need to go to school," Mom shouts.

I startle awake. My eyes are open, but my surroundings are unfamiliar. I don't know where I am, and I'm scared. It's dark, though some natural light filters into the room, lacking intensity like the sun is either rising or setting. I'm lying face-down, one eye open and one eye closed, pressed into the mattress. My arm hangs off the side of the bed. *How did I get here?*

It smells, but the aroma is unfamiliar. It's a mixture of dust and urine. The musk is almost overpowering as I inhale into the dirty mattress. I turn my head to the side and breathe the air in the room, stale and stagnant.

I push up on my elbow and look around. My head feels like it's in a fog. As if I'm King Tut waking from a thousand years of sleep or death. I move my arm, feeling a pinch. I look down, finding something connected to my forearm. A needle has been inserted with a tube extending up. I follow the tube from my arm into a transparent bag above my bed. *Am I in some kind of hospital? Did something happen to me?* I look to my right, surprised to find three other beds in the room. All are occupied by sleeping girls. They look young, my age. I don't recognize any, but one has a pool of vomit surrounding her.

I look down and notice I'm wearing a dress. The same dress I wore to the club. The club! My last memory is walking in the alley with David. I trusted him and left with him. He brought me to another man who covered my mouth and nose with a rag. The cloth had a smell I couldn't place. I felt something pierce my neck. Then everything went black.

My pulse is racing, and my chest is tight. I'm hyperventilating. I need to get out of here.

I move to swing my legs off the bed, but something holds me back. I look down and find a handcuff around my ankle. Its other end is attached to the frame of the bed. I panic. My breathing is shallow and rapid. Is it because of the lack of oxygen in the room or something else? My head is foggy. It's hard for me to think. *I'm going to die in here.*

I look around the room and notice a door. It's shut. It could be a closet, but it's the only door in the room. That's my way out if I can reach it. I slide down the bedside to examine the handcuffs. The cuff is too tight around my ankle. I try to slide it down my foot, but it barely moves and cuts across my skin. I gasp with pain. I'm not going to get it off.

I turn my attention to the cuff around the bed frame. This one is looser. I can slide it along the metal frame to the end of the bed, but that piece connects to the wooden endpiece. The frame is attached to the endpiece with a couple of screws. If I could get those loose, I'd be able to slide the cuff off the end, and I'd be free. I need a screwdriver. I press my thumb into the head of the screw, turning counterclockwise. Nothing. It won't budge.

I look up and see the same connection at the top of the bed. I slide my leg connected to the cuff up the bed until I reach the top. I can feel I've got a chance with this one. The screws are looser. I try the same thing with this one and my thumb. Nothing. I sit back on the bed in frustration. I scan the room, trying to find something that will act as a screwdriver. Nothing. My shoulders slump, and I feel the hope leaving me when I get an idea. I grasp the wood at the head of the bed and rock it back and forth. Alternating between pushing and pulling. It's not much, but there is a slight movement. I feel excitement as I look down at the screws connecting the frame. They seem to be moving. I push and pull harder, and the headboard knocks against the wall. It's not loud, but it's steady and consistent. After several vigorous pushes and pulls, the screws loosen. I reach down and can almost grasp their head between my fingers.

Just as I'm about to begin pushing and pulling again, I hear a click behind me. The handle of the door starts to turn. The door swings open, and a man a little older than me steps through. Our eyes lock. After several seconds he speaks, but it's in a language I can't understand. He's not speaking Hungarian or English. It sounds Slavic. Maybe Russian?

He recognizes I can't understand him and looks at the other girls. They're still sleeping, and he turns his attention back to me. As he comes closer, I recoil in fear. I push myself against the headboard. He walks to the bed, looking around. He's searching for something. *What is he looking for?* His searching stops as he looks at the bed-frame connected to the headboard. He says nothing, only smiles. It's a smile that chills my body. *What is he thinking? What does he plan to do?* I shrink from him in fear, but he doesn't hit me. He doesn't lay a finger on me. Instead, he checks the tube connected to my arm. He starts playing with it. Moving it. I feel cloudy again. He turns back to me and smiles as he waves goodbye. He moves to leave the room, but I'm not conscious long enough to see him go.

Chapter 12

Director Toth

I take a big bite of gyro, and just like always, I'm not disappointed. I love the lamb, feta cheese, sauce, and bread combination. My friend Németh László, mayor of Újpest, is late. We arranged to meet here, at Gyros Bros, for lunch. But I'm here, and he's not, and the smell of the food is too much for me. I'm not waiting for him as I take another bite. I can see László walking through the parking lot. His round body hustles to get inside.

He sees me and waves as he crosses the threshold of the door. I raise a pinky finger to him, my hands still around the large gyro. He steps to the counter and orders his food, then walks across the room toward the bank of windows and sits at the table across from me.

"Sorry, I'm late."

I take another bite of my gyro. I've never been a fan of tardiness, and he knows it.

"I got a call from Mádl Ferenc."

My eyebrows shoot up. "About what?"

Mádl Ferenc is the new president of the Republic of Hungary. His election was controversial since he doesn't belong to any particular political party. People have questioned how he garnered the support necessary to win. Some have even suggested polling fraud.

László taps on the table, leaning back in his chair. "He asked me to support his political agenda to reform the police force."

I stop in midchew, staring at him.

His eyes narrow, and he nods. "I thought you'd find that interesting."

I finish chewing, then set my gyro down and pick up a napkin. I wipe around my mouth and hands. "What reforms does he have in mind?"

"You aren't going to like it."

"I assumed that by the way you're acting. Try me."

László looks away, shaking his head. He's no longer making eye contact with me. "He says the increase in crime is tied to your leadership. He wants to make a change."

I nod, fighting to control the anger rising in me. László's food is ready, and he walks to the counter to retrieve it. It's true, crime has been on the rise in Budapest and the whole country. But that's not exclusive to us. Crime is on the rise in most former Eastern Bloc countries.

In truth, I've been worried about my job since President Mádl was elected. I became director of the Hungarian National Police by the nomination of Árpád Göncz, then-president of the republic. What I don't understand is, if Mádl intends to move against me, why tell László? We've been friends since childhood. Surely, he knows László would tell me.

László has his food and sits back down.

"What did you tell him?" I ask.

"What do you think I told him? I told him we've been friends since childhood, and no way I'd support him moving against you."

I nod and pat his hand. "Thank you."

"You're welcome. So, what are you going to do?"

I shake my head. "I'm not sure yet."

The mayor nods and leans toward me, dropping his voice. "Whatever you need, you know I have your back."

We lock eyes, and I nod.

He leans back and picks up his gyro. "Now, on to more important things, football. What needs to happen to fix the midfield problems of Újpest? We play Ferencváros tomorrow night."

I should have known he'd change the subject to football. He never misses an Újpest match. I've wondered if he only ran for mayor of district four to justify his football addiction.

For the next thirty minutes, we talk about football and the recently completed Summer Olympics in Sydney. Hungary took gold in men's water polo. Not bad for a country of only ten million people. I do my best to keep up with the conversation, but my mind remains on politics. Since taking the job, I've felt great pressure to reduce crime and make the country safer. The weight of the responsibility has now shifted from that of a gorilla to an elephant. If I hope to keep my job, I've got to turn up the heat and affect change quickly.

Chapter 13

Peter

"I've been wondering if I'd see you again."

Peter's sitting at the bar in Szépilona Bistro. Zsuzsa's back was to him, and she didn't see him come in. Surprise shows on her face when she notices him.

"It's good to see this place is still in business. I wondered if the door would be locked when I came over," Peter says.

Zsuzsa walks around the bar. Without a word, she throws her arms around him. Peter loves the feel of her body pressed to his. Letting go, she steps back and looks into his eyes. "How are you? Are you okay? I've been worried about you."

Peter sees the line on her forehead and the concern etched in the corners of her eyes. He can't help but be flattered.

"I worried about you too. I thought maybe I'd ruined your employment. Killing the founder and owner of the restaurant certainly isn't good for business. I'm glad the restaurant isn't closed, and you still have a job."

Zsuzsa shakes her head with an excited look in her eye. "Actually, it's much better now. Kata has taken over. I love her! She's so wonderful. She made me the manager."

Peter likes the happiness and relief in her eyes. The last time he had looked into those striking eyes, he saw fear. The restaurant was owned by Dobo Andras. Kata, Andras's wife, had suspected him of cheating and had hired Peter to investigate. During his investigation of Andras, Peter met Zsuzsa, the restaurant bartender. She had confided in him that Andras was much worse than a mere adulterer; he was involved in a human-trafficking ring. Peter followed Andras to his other restaurant in Croatia and learned Andras had abducted Kata, planning to kill her. Peter saved her and killed Andras on a train headed back to Budapest.

"I'm so happy for you, Zsuzsa. You deserve it. But what are you doing behind the bar if you're now the manager?"

She laughs, and Peter is reminded how loud her laugh can be. Several people turn to look at them. "I guess you can't take the bartender out of me so easily. Kata's here. She'd love to see you. Let me go get her."

Peter sits back down on the barstool and watches her walk to the office. After less than a minute, Kata comes out with Zsuzsa in tow. Her pace accelerates as she sees him. When she reaches him, she throws her arms around him, like Zsuzsa had. She kisses him on both cheeks, a sign of the affection she feels toward him.

Stepping back, she looks him up and down. "It's so good to see you. How are you?"

Peter can't help but wonder at the position he finds himself in. These women are beautiful and endure leering glances from men wherever they go, yet it's them looking at him.

"I'm good. I started working with the National Police. I'm helping to track down those responsible for the human trafficking here in Budapest."

Kata and Zsuzsa look at each other, and an unspoken message passes between them.

Kata says, "Peter, please be careful."

The concern he sees in their eyes is both comforting and disappointing. Do they not think he's capable of taking care of himself?

"Most of it is desk work. There's a whole group of us, and I'm the new kid on the block."

The women look unconvinced, but they don't push the issue further. An awkward silence falls, and Peter decides to bring a little levity. "So what's a guy got to do to get fed around here?"

Zsuzsa slaps him on the shoulder, and Kata laughs.

"Anything you want. And from now on, all your meals are on the house."

Peter shakes his head, about to object, when Zsuzsa steps forward and puts her hand over his mouth. "Would you rather sit at the bar or a table?"

Peter gives her a look but decides now isn't the time to argue and surveys the restaurant. He came to have a confidential conversation with them but is finding business is a bit too good. The restaurant is crowded for a weekday lunch. He notices a table close to a window, away from other patrons.

"How about over there?" he asks, pointing to the spot.

"Of course. Anywhere you like," Kata responds.

"Maybe you both could join me for a minute? There are a few things I'd like to discuss."

They look at each other, surprise registering. Kata leads Peter to the table, and Zsuzsa grabs a menu, three glasses, and some carbonated water.

After they all sit down, Kata turns to Peter. "So, what's on your mind?"

Peter takes a sip of water. "When we were in Croatia, you asked me how Andras got into trafficking. I didn't know and still don't. Have you learned anything since?"

Kata takes a deep breath and shrugs. "Yes and no." She looks out the window. "I've thought about little else since that horrible night when he beat me and put me in that produce truck. I can't get over how you think you know someone and then learn they're someone else entirely. I think back over the last couple of years, searching for clues. I can't come up with much. I was naïve, obviously." She chuckles and looks at them. Zsuzsa nods in support. Kata looks back out the window. "But there is one thing I'm sure of." She turns her head, looking Peter in the eye. "You might not like to hear it. But I think you need to."

Peter's taken aback. He had asked the question, why wouldn't he want to hear it?

"I'm convinced there's corruption in the police force. Somebody on the inside was feeding him information, and he used it to his benefit. I'm not sure who or what their role is, but he knew things he shouldn't."

Zsuzsa nodded but no longer in support. Was it because they had discussed it before? Or did she know it also?

"Like what?" Peter asks.

"For one, he knew who the next mayor would be even before the election. And I'm not just talking about being connected. He *knew it*. It was like he was assured that no matter how the election turned out, Mayor Zsigmond would be mayor." She shakes her head and taps her long fingernails on the table. "You remember when I hired you? I knew something was wrong. I thought he was cheating on me, and he probably was. But regardless, I had a feeling things weren't right, even though I had no proof. He was too good at covering his tracks. Just like I knew something was wrong, I knew he was working with the police. He had such confidence. Don't get me wrong. He was always confident. But this was even more. He knew things."

"I know what you mean," Zsuzsa says. "One time, outside the restaurant, I saw him talking to a tall man. I had come out the back door, right over there." She points to the kitchen. "I wasn't expecting anyone to be there. There's Andras and the man talking. As soon as they saw me, the man said something to Andras and left. He wasn't blocking his face, but it was obvious he didn't want to be recognized. He got in a government-issued vehicle and drove away."

"How'd you know it was a government-issued vehicle?" Peter asks.

"The plates."

Peter listens to both women, absently rubbing his beard. None of this comes as a surprise. He had harbored suspicions but never voiced them. These stories only strengthened them.

"If I were to show you a picture of the man you saw him with, could you recognize him?"

Zsuzsa works her mouth and shakes her head. "I don't know. It wasn't long, and he was wearing a hat. I didn't get a good look at him." She jumps up from the table. "Your food is probably done. Let me go grab it."

He hadn't ordered anything yet, but he isn't surprised when Zsuzsa returns with a heaping plate of beef stroganoff. He had raved about this meal since the first time he'd had it here. Peter can't hide the happiness he feels, and both women laugh at the expression on his face.

"I think everyone in Budapest knows how much you like it," Zsuzsa says.

He chuckles. It's true. He had told people about the food here, especially the stroganoff.

She also sets down a foaming mug of Dreher beer. Both women say, "Jó éjt vágyat."

As he begins eating, Kata leans close to whisper, "Do you know where the trafficking is happening now?"

Peter nods. "We have some leads, but I shouldn't say anything. It's an ongoing investigation."

The women look at each other.

"Zsuzsa, before you worked here, I remember you said you worked at a club in the city. What was the club's name?" he asks.

"Ötkert."

Peter can't hide the surprise in his eyes.

"Is that where it's happening?" Zsuzsa asks.

Peter shakes his head. He's already said too much. "I didn't say that." He didn't have to. They both knew.

"Well, I still know the manager there. He's always trying to get me to come back and work on the weekends to help with the rush. I guess it's become trendy. I could help you."

The stroganoff is unbelievably delicious, and he's going at it with some ferocity. But this turn in the conversation slows him. He sits back in the chair, looking at them.

"How?" he asks.

Zsuzsa looks at Kata, and again an unspoken conversation passes between them. "I could help out on weekends. Be undercover for you."

Peter shakes his head. "No."

"I'm just saying, I can bartend. I won't do anything. I'll just pay attention. See if I notice anything unusual."

"You were here with Andras. You know how scary these traffickers can be. I remember the night you told me about him. You were beyond scared. How long did you live in fear for your life? I'm not going to put you back in that situation again."

Now it's Kata who speaks. "Peter, you need help to solve this. She's just going to bartend. She won't do anything stupid. She worked with Andras for years and never had any problems. She'll be safe."

Peter knows there's little point in arguing. This is a battle he isn't going to win.

Chapter 14

Peter

The lights of Budapest are beautiful any time of year, but near Christmas, they seem endless. Anywhere Peter looks from the window of the streetcar, he sees red and green illumination. The streetcar will soon depart Moskva Square and head east toward the river. Moskva Square is the central public transportation hub on the Buda side of the city. At Moskva, trains, streetcars, buses, and a subway converge. Eventually, any public transportation on the Buda side of the city passes through Moskva. After talking with Kata and Zsuzsa, Peter takes a bus down from Szépilona Bistro. He climbs on the streetcar, picking a spot in the middle. The weather is nice, considering it's December in Budapest, but now the sun is gone, and the air has a bite to it. His spot in the middle of the car shields him from the arctic blast entering at each stop.

After a few stops, they begin to cross to the Pest side of the city via the Margit Bridge, which boasts one of Peter's favorite views of the city. Riding along the tracks, one gets a view of the castle in the Buda hills, Gellert Hill in the distance, and multiple bridges, including the Chain Bridge. He could have taken the subway, it's faster, but he's in no rush. Only a cold, empty apartment awaits him. Plus, he needs time to think. His thoughts always flow best while moving.

The revelation that Zsuzsa knows the manager of the Ötkert Club both surprised and excited him. The prospect of her working there scares him. Since losing his wife over a year ago, Zsuzsa had been his only date. He always had a great time with her. Perhaps, he enjoyed it too much. He liked her, and it alarmed him. It felt like cheating on his wife. A nagging sense of guilt crept up each time he laughed. When he kissed her, it compounded the tumult of emotion. He still belongs to his wife. Spending time with another woman felt wrong.

His meeting with Zsuzsa had been happenstance. She was a bartender working in Andras's restaurant. Peter had been drawn to her from the moment he saw her. He moved from a table to the bar, hoping to strike up a conversation and glean information. No, it wasn't just about investigation. He wanted to be nearer to her. He was surprised when she flirted with him, and he couldn't help but flirt back. They had gone on a short, spark-filled date, and Zsuzsa had confided her fears about Andras. From that point, Peter left for Croatia, and they lost touch. It had been several weeks since he had seen her, but seeing her today only added to his confusion.

On the one hand, he wanted her. He wanted to be with her. He felt himself longing for her. On the other, was he betraying Karen? If he was being honest, it didn't just scare him because of Karen. A relationship with him had proven to be dangerous. His wife had been murdered, and although Peter had never confirmed it, he was confident it was an act of revenge on him. He would never forgive himself for not seeing it. For not protecting her.

The streetcar bell rouses him from his thoughts. They've reached Szent Istvan, his stop. Peter exits and walks south toward his apartment. He lives near Váci Utca, the major shopping street in Budapest. No cars are allowed on the road, and shops and cafes line the street. It's a major tourist attraction, complete with overpriced merchandise. Typically, the road is full of pedestrians. But not tonight. It's quiet. Shopping isn't as popular in the cold and dark.

After a ten-minute walk, Peter enters his apartment building. His cheeks and nose are bright red from the cold. He climbs two flights of stairs, but before reaching his apartment, he hears a young voice call out, "Kezét csókolom."

He turns to see Judith, his nine-year-old neighbor, waving to him. She's wearing pajamas and has her long blond hair bunched on top of her head. Seeing her buoys his spirits. In a way, it makes him feel like he isn't alone. Behind the door, he hears her mother call her back in, and they wave before she shuts the door. Peter turns to his door and opens it stepping inside. The loneliness cuts through him like a knife. He doesn't know if he will ever not think about her when he arrives home. Sometimes he imagines this not being real. Karen is waiting for him, sitting on the couch or cooking in the kitchen. He comes in, and she gets to her feet. He sees the love in her eyes. She comes to him, expecting a kiss. He wraps her in his arms, pleased to fulfill her expectation.

But instead, he flips on the lights walking down the hall to his office. Kovacs knew he was going to talk with Zsuzsa and Kata, and he'd want a report. Peter slumps down in his chair, picks up the phone, and dials Kovacs at the office. The answering machine picks up. Peter considers leaving a message and calling it a day. But he knows Kovacs is anxious for news, no matter the time. Checking his notebook, he dials his home number. After a few rings, Kovacs's wife answers. After exchanging pleasantries with Peter, she tells him she'll get Lajos.

"Peter?"

"Yes, it's me."

"How'd it go?"

Peter tells him about seeing Kata and Zsuzsa, how Zsuzsa knew the club's manager, and how he's always trying to get her to help during the weekends. He doesn't tell him that both Zsuzsa and Kata are convinced that Andras had an informant in the police force. Peter decides to keep that to himself, not yet knowing who he can trust.

"How would she feel about taking the manager up on the offer? It would be nice to have someone working inside that club. If we were to plant someone randomly, that could take weeks."

"Actually, she suggested it. She wants to do it."

"But you don't want her to?"

"No."

"Why not?"

"Because it could be dangerous. She already went through a risky situation with Andras."

Kovacs pauses. "I agree, she did. But that's also why I'd like to see her do it. She handled Andras's situation well."

Peter knows he's right. Andras had been a dangerous man, but he had never harmed Zsuzsa, even when she had questioned him.

"We'll only let her stay in there for a weekend or two. We'll tell her not to ask any questions, just observe."

Peter still has an unsettled feeling but agrees. After they hang up, Peter walks into the kitchen, fills his kettle, and lights the stove. Sitting down at the kitchen table, he waits for the water to boil. His stomach is in knots. He knows the tea will do little to settle his ache.

Chapter 15

Zsuzsa

"Zsuzsa, this is Csaba. You two will be working together tonight."

It's early, six p.m. The club manager, Agoston, shows me around and introduces me to my new coworkers. Csaba, the other bartender, is a handsome man in a white shirt and black tie. He's young, probably twenty-five or so, ten years younger than me. At first, he looks me in the eye, but his eyes quickly lower to my chest and remain there.

He extends his hand. "Zsuzsa, nice to meet you."

I take his hand. It's warm and firm. He smiles, showing a slight crowding of teeth along the bottom, but besides that, a nice smile.

"Pleased to meet you, Csaba."

"I understand you used to work here."

"Yes, although it's been a long time. I've been in a restaurant for the last several years. Much slower paced."

Agoston turns away, wanting to continue the tour.

"Well, nice to meet you, Csaba. I look forward to working with you."

"You too, Zsuzsa."

Agoston continues to lead me around the club, introducing me to people. I only catch a quarter of the names and feel a little overwhelmed. It's been a long time since I started a new job, and even though I have a ton of experience and have even worked here before, I can't help feeling anxiety about whether I can keep up. I'm not as young as I was then.

Agoston stops in front of a kid. At least he looks like a kid. He can't be older than sixteen. "Zsuzsa, this is Bela," he says, motioning toward the kid. He's small, maybe only my height, and thin. He can't be much over a hundred pounds. He smiles, and it's kind of a goofy smile. Something isn't quite right about it. I think it might be the gap between his teeth. He meets my eyes, then lets his gaze fall to my chest. There's an awkward silence as the kid stares at my boobs.

"Hey, Bela." Agoston snaps his fingers in front of him. "I said, this is Zsuzsa."

Bela seems to emerge from his motorboating trance. He extends his hand, not even looking at me, clearly embarrassed to have been caught. But I don't care. I'm used to this. Since I was a teenage girl, men have leered at my body. I've got a great rack, and I'm not going to wear loose-fitting clothing to avoid the eyeballs. I'll wear what I want. Let them look. Sometimes I use it to my advantage. I wear tight tops with cleavage when I work. Men, and sometimes even women, seem more generous then.

"Nice to meet you, Bela. I'm Zsuzsa." I smile, showing him I don't mind that he was caught looking. He turns to the side, trying to hide his embarrassment and maybe something else. As he shakes my hand, he gives me a cautious smile, and I see him sneak another peek. It makes me laugh.

Agoston shakes his head. He seems more embarrassed than the kid. "Bela, will you show Zsuzsa the wine cellar?" He turns back to me. "Sorry, I have a few things to take care of before we open. Bela's the bar porter. He'll be able to show you around and answer your questions. Once you're done, make your way to the bar. Csaba will show you the ropes."

He leaves, and I'm left waiting on Bela. He watches Agoston walk away, then turns back to me. Again, I catch him sneaking a peek, but I pretend not to notice.

"So, are you going to show me the wine cellar, or what?"

Bela's cheeks color, and he nods. He gestures toward the hallway on our left. "I guess he wants me to show you where the wine cellar is."

Uh... yeah, kid. That's precisely what he said.

I fall in step beside him as he walks toward the hallway. Something about the kid makes me want to treat him like a little brother. Tease him a bit.

"So, Bela, how long have you been working here?"

"About a year."

He doesn't give me more than that. I can see a long, philosophical discussion isn't in our immediate future.

"Why do you want to work in a club? For the alcohol?"

He looks at me and shakes his head. "No, I don't drink much."

"Oh, it must be to stare at all the pretty girls then."

He looks away and turns red but then sees I'm smiling. He realizes he's being teased and ducks his head. "Maybe."

I laugh, and my outburst echoes through the hallway. I pat him on the shoulder. "Don't worry, I won't judge. Sometimes I like to look also."

He shoots me a sideways glance that makes me laugh harder. I'm going to have fun with this kid. We reach the end of the hallway. He takes out his keys and opens the door. Behind the door is a narrow stairwell. We head down a couple flights of stairs, and I can feel the temperature drop. I wonder if it's really getting colder or if it's just my imagination. The air feels damp.

"This is where the wine cellar is. You need a key to open this door and the one we came in upstairs."

I guess, in his mind, all women with big boobs are stupid. I watched him get the keys out and open the door. He repeats the action at the cellar door, and we go in. It's not just my imagination. It's definitely colder in here. He flips on the light, and wine racks, cataloged by year and type, appear. Bela points out different wines as if I've never been in a wine cellar before. At the end of his little tour, he shows me where we must log any wine taken from the basement. Several sheets sit on a clipboard on a desk in the corner. As I scrutinize the list, Bela becomes tense. He leans over and takes the clipboard from my hands.

"Come on. We need to get back upstairs."

"Okay."

He nearly shoves me out of the room. We make our way back up the stairs and through the hallway. When we reach the dance floor, he points to the bar, and I see Csaba.

"I have to do a few things now. Agoston wants you to help out Csaba."

"Thanks for the tour. I look forward to working with you more."

He nods and heads off as I walk toward Csaba. He thinks I missed it, and maybe I should let him. But I know what he didn't want me to see. The club has a wine thief.

Chapter 16

Zsuzsa

"Zsuzsa, will you go in the back and get more of the Tokaji red?"

I barely hear him over the music and voices. Csaba is busy mixing a drink and isn't looking at me as he barks. He holds up the wine bottle, showing me it's empty. The request is an order, not a question. He continues fulfilling requests, never glancing in my direction.

I push down the irritation as I struggle to make my way out of the bar. It's Saturday night in the club, and young, attractive people are everywhere. To get more wine, I have to swim through a sea of gyrating twenty-somethings, through the dark hall, and down several flights of stairs to the dank wine cellar. Can't someone else do it? Where's Bela? Isn't this *his* job?

Csaba knows my experience level. He knows better than to treat me like this. I'm a bartender, not a bar porter. This isn't my first rodeo. I've been tending bar for over twelve years now. I was a bartender here while he was still pulling girls' pigtails in the schoolyard. Yes, I haven't been bartending in a club for a long time, and this is my first week back, but it's like riding a bike. I'm ten times the bartender he is. He should be learning from me.

As I clear the dance floor, I inhale. The change of temperature in the hallway is palpable. It's a reprieve. I hadn't realized how hot it was and how much I felt the constant thump of the music. A little distance is pleasant. *What if I didn't go back*? It's not like I need this job. In fact, I don't want it. I'm only doing this for Peter. He needs my help, and there isn't much I wouldn't do for him. I can't understand the gravitational pull he has on me. At the very thought of helping him, I would swim across the ocean. I've never felt that way about a man.

I reach the end of the hall, open the door, and navigate the stairs. The stairway is narrow, and I've got to watch my step. I'd hate to snag a heel, tumble face-first into a wall, and roll to the bottom of the stairs. That kind of fall could seriously hurt somebody. The jagged rock walls feel cold and unforgiving as I run my hand along them for support. My frustration with Bela builds with each step. *Where is he, anyway*? The kid seems to disappear without any reason.

Reaching the cement floor at the bottom, I can barely hear the music above. The cellar feels like climbing into the center of the earth. It's musty, damp, and cold. Pulling out the key, I shove it in the lock and twist. The door slips open, and I'm staring into the dark. I hate this part, groping for the switch along the wall. It feels like a game of cat and mouse where I'm unsure if I'm the cat or the mouse. That's a bad analogy. There are probably mice down here. I feel something run along my toe, and I scream.

My hand brushes up and down the wall. I almost give up and turn back when I feel the switch and lever it up. The light blinks and comes alive with a slight buzz. It's surprising how extensive this cellar is. There are at least a hundred wine racks, with many wrapping around the corner into the darker area. I haven't been back there and don't plan to go. I can only imagine what lurks there.

Tokaji red is one of the most popular wines in the club. That demand should keep it near the front. I peruse the racks. Within seconds I find it. I grab two bottles, hoping that will be enough, and make my way to the door. I set down the bottles, turn out the lights, and begin to shut the door when I hear a sound. I look up. The sound is coming from above. *Did I hear what I thought I heard*? I release my grip on the doorknob. I'm not moving now, listening.

There it is again. It sounds like a muffled scream. The scream gives way to the sound of loud steps and shuffling. Almost like someone is being dragged down the stairs. It's coming closer. *What do I do*? I look around wildly. My stomach drops, and I feel panic rising. There isn't anywhere to hide. I'll be found.

The sound of shuffling feet stops.

"What's wrong with her?" a deep voice asks.

"She's having a seizure," another voice responds.

"What should we do?"

There's a long pause before the other one speaks.

"Let's take her back."

They turn around and head back up the stairs. Their footsteps grow fainter. Then I hear the door above close. I let out my breath. I realize I'm trembling. *What was that*? Maybe it was just people in the club? I'm anxious to get back behind the bar now. I close the door, lock it, and head back up the stairs.

Chapter 17

David

I'm the one who does all the dangerous work, yet I get paid little.

Maybe *dangerous* isn't the correct term. The work isn't hazardous. It's not like anyone is tracking me. It's more that I'm the only guy who could do this. I'm a savant. I'm a talent that they underappreciate. It doesn't hurt that women can't seem to take their eyes off me. But it's so much more than that. These girls love to be the focus of a man's attention, and I know how to give them what they want. Who else has the skills I have? Movie-star good looks, intelligence, charisma. These girls don't stand a chance.

That's why it makes me so angry. How can Agoston not see it? No, he sees it. He just doesn't appreciate it. Maybe I should go away for a bit. Make him realize how much he needs me. He'd be sunk without me. His boss would be so angry. The guy nobody knows, only Agoston. Whoever he is, he wields a lot of power. Agoston is terrified of the guy. He'll do anything he's told. Well, not me. I'm tired of being taken for granted. After tonight, I'm going to talk to Agoston. Tell him how it is. If they don't pay, I walk. And if I walk, good luck to them finding anyone even close to as skilled. I'm perfect for this role.

I look out over the dance floor, seeking my next prey. I have a sixth sense for it. I'm a master at spotting the girls. The ones ripe for the taking. It's hard to even describe how I know. There aren't any telltale signs. Instead, it's almost a feeling. The way they carry themselves. It's not like I have a type. In fact, that's another of my gifts. I'm able to attract them all. Variety is the name of this game. Most buyers don't want the same. Sure, they have a type. All men do. But it's often variety in those types. Nobody wants a Barbie all the time.

Scanning the floor, my eyes fall on one particular beauty. I've seen her before. I think she's been here a couple of nights, actually. She always keeps to herself. She looks like she wants to get out and dance but never does. She hangs back, clutching her wine glass. Seemingly gaining courage from it. Hoping and praying a man might come and sweep her off her feet.

Usually, I would never approach her. I don't like a girl who's been here before. I want someone new, someone out of her comfort zone. They're easier to win over. They long for it. But this girl is still nervous. She needs someone to rescue her. She's young, maybe not as young as I would normally like. But again, a little variety is good, even with age. She's wearing a light white dress with spaghetti straps. It's low on her chest, highlighting her ample breasts. I like her. I like the way her dress clings to her hips.

I stand and move toward her. She's maybe forty feet away, which gives me plenty of time to plan my attack. The game always includes a method. Which method is going to appeal to her? It depends on the prey. Some girls love the arrogant man. The man they feel they have to pursue. They want to feel like they leveled up. Got someone out of their league. They need an ego boost. Some like the sweet man. The man who dotes on them and praises their every feature and movement. They also need an ego boost but in a different way. They need to feel wanted. Still, others like the successful man. The man who seems to have so much going for him. They want a man who will take care of them. What man will she respond to? Let's find out.

"I've seen you in here before?" I say to her as I approach.

She's leaning against a high table with her drink in her hand. She has to turn to look at me, making eye contact. Thinking I might not be talking to her, she looks behind herself. Checking to be sure. Her eyes lower, and her long lashes cover her eyes. She likes the attention, but she's scared of it.

"Yeah, I've been here a couple of times."

Her voice is sweet but cautious. A hint of a smile plays at her lips, and her eyes sparkle as she looks up at me. She loves that I've noticed her. She seems to be alone; I love that.

I look into her eyes. "I noticed you the first time you came. I hoped you'd come back." She looks down, and her cheeks color. "I had to make sure you didn't have a boyfriend."

Although I'm almost positive she doesn't, I throw that out early to make sure. I don't need a crazy boyfriend coming after me or looking for her. I need someone who won't be immediately missed.

Her cheeks color again before she tells me she doesn't, but she wishes she did.

"A woman as intoxicating as you? You could have your pick. They're just afraid to approach you. They don't want to be rejected."

She smiles, and something in the way she holds her breath tells me she's had this same thought. She's wondered why men don't talk to her much. "Is that what it is?" she asks me coyly. "I don't bite." She smiles a delicious smile. "Hard, anyway." She laughs an embarrassed laugh and puts her hand over her mouth.

She's a lot more fun than I expected. I take her cue and step up my own game. I move in closer, whispering in her ear. "You can bite me anywhere you like, as long as you kiss it better afterward."

She turns her body standing in front of me now. The tip of her tongue slides along her lips. The message is clear. I lean down and put my lips on hers. Strawberry? Cherry? Her lips are soft. Her tongue extends and meets mine. There's no doubt she wants this.

These are the times I hate my job. I wish I could take her and give her what she wants. But I can't. It's not allowed. If I seduce these eager young girls, I'm not allowed to play with them. Sometimes I can't wait to pass them off. They can be annoying. Talking too much about who knows what. Other times, like this, it's torture. I crave them. My hands are on her back, and I'm pulling her to me. I don't have to pull hard; she's anxious to press her body against mine. I feel my own excitement and know I'm playing with fire. I need to do my job and turn her over.

After a minute of kissing and groping, I release her lips. I turn my head, my lips running along the side of her neck. She's holding her breath, enjoying the feeling. I move my mouth to her ear. "Let's go somewhere a little more private."

She looks at me, and although apprehensive, she agrees. I take her hand, guiding her across the dance floor toward the back hallway. As we clear the hordes of people, I put my arm around her, and she snuggles in against me. I open the emergency exit at the end of the hall, and we feel the cold air. It's refreshing at first, but not after the heat of the club has worn off.

In the dark alleyway, I see Ferenc's taillights. I'm tempted to turn the other way. Keep this girl for me. But we continue walking. Her body pressed to mine. At least the car will be warm.

We're close now, maybe ten paces. I can see and smell the glow of his cigarette. As he turns toward me, I'm surprised to see his attention isn't on us. It's behind us. He's not leering at the girl. I stop, turning to look. As I do, I hear the squeal of tires. Ferenc speeds away. *What's going on?* I move forward, preparing to run after him when I hear it. The click of a gun hammer. It's pressed to my temple. "You're under arrest."

Chapter 18

Peter

Peter looks through the one-sided window at the handsome man seated at the table. His hands are still cuffed behind his back. Peter can't help thinking the guy looks like Keanu Reeves. Not *Bill and Ted's Excellent Adventure* Keanu. That's too young. More like *Point Break* Reeves. Peter's only vaguely following the conversation behind him when he hears his name.

"Peter, why don't you take the lead in interviewing him."

He sees that Kovacs has turned toward him, holding up his hand at Szabo and the others as they begin to protest. The request surprises Peter. He assumed Kovacs would handle it. But almost as quickly, he sees the wisdom of it. Kovacs arrested him. A change of face might make him more comfortable. Peter agrees and moves toward the door.

Szabo steps in front of him. "Don't screw this up, Peter."

Peter has to push past him to leave the room. The younger man's head comes up as he enters. His eyebrows rise in surprise, obviously not expecting a new person. Peter walks behind him, unlocking his handcuffs. The man exhales, wincing from the pain of moving his arms. He windmills them back and forth, trying to get some blood flow. Peter picks the chair next to him, preferring to be close.

"It's about time," the young man says.

"My name is Andrassy Peter. And you are?"

The man looks at him warily. "You can call me Gyula."

Interesting. Another name. And perhaps even more interesting, the man knows they confiscated his ID. They know exactly who he is, yet he believes he can still lie.

"Okay, Gyula. Thanks for coming to meet with me tonight."

He chuckles. "Like I had any choice. I didn't even do anything."

"Oh, well, if that's the case, then all you have to do is answer some questions, and we can get you on your way. What took you to the club tonight?"

"I went to relax. Have a few drinks. Maybe find some cute girls. Is that a crime?" He waves his arms, motioning around the room. "If so, I should be surrounded by other criminals in here."

"What kinds of girls do you like?"

He looks at Peter as if he's daft. "Pretty ones, duh."

"Like the girl you were leaving the club with?"

"Yep. And you guys ruined it. She was hot, man."

"What did we ruin?"

Gyula smiles. "You know what you ruined. We were headed back to my apartment." He makes a circle with one hand and extends his other finger through it over and over. He laughs too loudly. It's all Peter can do not to stand up and punch the guy in the face.

"A handsome guy like you. I'm sure you'll get more chances."

He shrugs. "Yeah, but not with her. You scared her off."

Little did he know she was undercover. Varga had graduated at the top of her class and was well trained. She could have torn him apart.

"Do you go to that club often?"

"I've only been a couple of times."

"Really? Only a couple?"

His eyes narrow at Peter. "Yes, only a couple."

Peter holds a clipboard. He pretends to look down and read something on it. "That's funny. We have multiple witnesses who say you're there almost every night."

The man's cheeks color, and he strums his fingers on the table. "Okay, so what. Maybe I do go to the club a lot. Is that a crime?"

Peter shakes his head. "Not a crime. But those same witnesses claim you sit in the same booth every night. You almost always leave with a new woman draped around you."

He smiles a lip-splitting smile. "What can I say? The girls love me. I shouldn't be arrested for that. What, an old dude like you, you're jealous? They don't even look at you anymore, huh?"

Peter laughs. "No, that's not a crime either." He leans forward and slaps the table, making Gyula jump. His demeanor has gone from curiosity to anger. "But what happens to those girls, Gyula? Nobody sees them in the club again. Nobody sees them at all."

The color drains from his face now. But he does his best to hide it. "I guess once they've been with me, nothing else compares. They don't want to go back."

"Or they can't because they've been abducted. Is that what would have happened to the girl tonight? Was she going to disappear in that car in the alley? Never to be seen again."

"No."

"Well, that's not what the bartender says."

"Csaba?"

"Yeah, Csaba says you," Peter looks down at his clipboard pretending to read something, "David. You're the guy who meets the girls and takes them out back to the alleyway. Some other guy drugs them and takes them away."

He's quiet now. All of his bravado has flown out of the room. When he speaks, his words are pleading.

"Look, I never did anything to any of those girls. I just dropped them off. That was it."

"Who hired you?"

He shakes his head. "I can't tell you that. He'll kill me."

Peter decides to make him think a little more. "How old are you?"

Gyula looks surprised by the turn in the conversation. "I'm twenty-six."

Peter nods. "You love that women look at you, right? Love how they turn and stare at you when you enter a room? You love the effect you have on them. It feels good. Do you think you'll still impact them when you're thirty years older? When you get out of prison after thirty long, hard years? Do you think life will be good then?"

David's breathing speeds up, growing shallow. His cheeks fill with color. "Look, man, his name is Agoston, all right? He's the manager of the club. He hired me. He told me all he needed me to do was get these girls to walk out with me to the alleyway behind the club. Get them alone. He'd give me descriptions of what they should look like. I just got them to leave with me, then turn them over to a guy waiting for them in the alley. That's all I did. And they paid me good money for it."

"Where did the girls go from there? Where would he take them?"

"I don't know. They didn't tell me, and I didn't ask. I didn't really want to know."

Peter puts his hands on the table and leans forward. "I don't know if I can trust you, Gyula. Or should I call you Vik? Or maybe David? Or perhaps even your real name, József. You could see how you might not be that trustworthy."

He put his hands up in the air. "I swear. I don't know where the girls went. Only Agoston knows that. And his boss."

Peter raises an eyebrow. "What do you mean, *his boss*? Who's his boss?"

He shakes his head. "I don't know. I never saw him. But whoever he is, Agoston is terrified of him. He gets his orders from him."

Chapter 19

Peter

"József said there were more girls taken this week. Not just Renata. That needs to be the priority. We need to find them before they're gone for good."

Detective Kovacs Lajos stands in front of the human-trafficking task force. Peter and the other three sit at the table listening to him. Peter agrees with him but knows it's going to be tough. József claimed not to know what happened to the girls after he'd brought them to the guy in the alley, and Peter believed him.

"How are we going to do that? We don't even know where they are." Szabo had obviously been thinking the same thing. "We shouldn't have arrested József when we did. We should have let Varga be taken. Follow her and find out where they take the girls. Varga could have handled herself."

Peter looks to the side and sees Varga nod. What's this connection between Szabo and Varga? Doesn't she know what a dufus he is?

When to arrest him had been a hot topic among the task force members before placing Varga undercover. She and Szabo had argued they needed to wait and let her be taken. Kovacs decided to protect Varga rather than let her be abducted. He didn't want to risk losing her and adding another victim to the list. Szabo had eventually seen the logic and agreed with Kovacs. Now he seems to have changed his mind. Szabo would probably have a different take if József knew where the girls had gone. Hindsight was twenty-twenty. Peter couldn't blame Kovacs for making the call he did. If Varga had been taken by the traffickers and they lost her, it would weigh heavy on all their consciences.

"Well, Szabo, if you were in charge of the task force, you could have made that call. But instead, it's me, and I made the best decision possible, given the circumstances. I also remember you agreeing with that course of action before we did it."

Peter loves that Kovacs calls him out. A lesser leader might not have the stones. Peter's esteem for Kovacs moves up another notch.

"You can hardly blame them," Szabo says.

Kovacs stares at him, not following. "Blame who?"

"The traffickers. You can't blame them for taking the girls. The way they dress. Some of these girls are just asking for it."

Peter can't believe his ears. He looks at Kovacs and sees the same dumbfounded expression on his face.

"You think because they dress provocatively, they deserve to be taken from their homes and families and sold into slavery?" Peter would prefer to hold his tongue in these types of meetings, letting Kovacs handle it. But this comment disgusts him too much.

Szabo turns to Peter; a look crosses his face like he knows he went too far, but he isn't smart enough to apologize. "No, I'm not saying they should be taken. I'm just saying some of them seem to be asking for it." His voice lowers. A pin dropping in the room would sound like a dump truck in a nitroglycerine plant. Everyone holds their breath.

Finally, Kovacs clears his throat. "I'm going to pretend you never said that." He looks around, making eye contact with each group member. "I think we all should." His eyes turn to Szabo. "But I never want to hear an opinion like that again. Do you understand me?"

Szabo looks up and mumbles something while nodding. Peter looks at Varga; she hasn't reacted. She can't have liked his comment.

Kovacs looks away, disgust evident on his face. He paces over to the window. They all look away from Szabo and focus on Kovacs.

"All right, what do we know?" Kovacs stares out the window, thinking out loud. "József has been meeting girls in the club and getting them to follow him. He turns them over to a guy in the alley, and the guy takes them away. The manager, Agoston, hired him to meet and deliver the girls." He turns back to the group and begins pacing again. "We know Agoston isn't working alone. We know he's working for someone else. Someone who seems to be connected. Someone he fears. We know Renata was taken, and several other girls. All of them are either foreign or from the country, outside Budapest. Like Andras, they prey on those with few connections."

Kovacs takes a breath as if he has more to say but stops. After a short pause, he speaks again. His words indicate he's accepted their fate. "The club is no longer a good spot for us. I don't believe they'll be brash enough to continue operations there. They'll move on, at least for a while. I'm afraid we're back to square one. Szabo, Varga, and Farkas, our only hope now is finding the manager. Work together to see what you can learn about this Agoston fella, and see if you can find him. Take as many uniformed police officers as you can. Turn the city upside down if you have to, but find him. Once we have him, we're going to lean on him—hard. We'll get him to talk." He turns to Peter. "You and I are going to start interviewing friends and families of other victims. Maybe we can learn something from them. Identify a pattern."

Chapter 20

Peter

Peter sits at his desk in the bullpen on the second floor of the Hungarian National Police Headquarters. He has a stack of files in front of him. Following their meeting with the rest of the task force, Kovacs pulled him aside and asked if he would look at the other missing girl files. All who had gone missing over the last few months. Kovacs hoped a fresh set of eyes might discover something, see something he had missed. This was work Peter had done a million times as a detective in New York City. The Hungarian files were different, mainly in language and formatting. But the pertinent information was still inside. Each one contained an intake form, probably completed by a uniformed officer, a photo or photos, transcripts of interviews conducted with friends and family, and notes from other detectives.

After looking at several files, Peter has an idea. He counts twelve files on his desk. He takes out a sheet of paper and draws lines from top to bottom as straight as he can. He then turns the sheet to the side and makes ten straight lines roughly an inch apart, forming even-sized boxes across the whole sheet. In the top compartments of each column, he writes the names of each girl. Along the left, he writes different personal characteristics, like birthplace, hair color, age, height, weight, last place seen, home address, etc. He spends the next hour filling in the information, not sure what the result will be, but wanting a single place to profile each victim.

After completing his chart, he reviews the information. The physical characteristics of each victim are all over the map. They took blondes and brunettes, girls with green eyes and brown. The missing women are tall and short, ranging in age from eighteen to twenty-four. The traffickers have no "type." They like variety. Next, he begins analyzing the birthplaces and family sizes of each. Again, there's no correlation between victims and their backgrounds. Finally, he looks at the last location seen. At first glance, this is a bust also, but something catches his eye. It's the roman numeral at the end of each address. The last twelve missing girls have been abducted in the same district in Budapest. *Could this be right?*

Peter double-checks his chart against each file. It's correct. This can't be a coincidence. There are twenty-three districts in Budapest. No way they can all be from the same district out of coincidence. And that's just the last twelve missing women. Maybe there are more? Peter stands and walks to Kovacs's office. He knocks on the closed door, waiting for a reply. Hearing voices in the room, he turns away, planning to return. He stops when Kovacs calls out, "Come in." Peter turns back and opens the door. He's surprised to see Director Toth sitting on the metal chair across from Kovacs.

"Oh, I'm sorry. I'll come back later." He moves to close the door.

"Peter, I was updating the director on our investigation," Kovacs says.

"Sorry to interrupt. I'll come back later."

"Nonsense," the director says. "Come and take a seat." He pats the arm of the chair next to him. Peter obliges, sitting down across the desk from Kovacs. Kovacs comes around the desk, closes the door, and retakes his seat.

"I just finished telling the director about your interview with József."

The director nods. "Sounds like you did a good job. You gained some valuable information from him. Too bad our cover is blown in the club, though."

The director glares at Kovacs, and Kovacs drops his eyes. Peter hates that Kovacs is being blamed for protecting another agent and possible victim.

"I actually have some good news on that front," Peter says.

The director turns his attention to Peter.

"Lajos asked me to review the files of the last twelve abducted girls. He said he had a hunch they had something in common."

The director glances back at Kovacs, and although Kovacs hadn't said that, he doesn't argue.

"Anyway, I did what he asked and compared the profiles of each victim. It turns out they were all taken in the same district in Budapest. Or at least, that's the last place they were seen."

"Really?" the director says.

Peter nods, and Kovacs smiles.

"Which district?" Kovacs asks.

"The fourth," Peter tells him.

Kovacs shakes his head. "I wonder what the significance of that is."

"What do you think it tells us, Peter?" the director asks.

"I think it shows us these girls weren't picked at random. They were seen in the district. Our traffickers are operating exclusively in District Four for some reason."

They all sit back in their chairs. Kovacs shakes his head. "Wait, but József brought Renata to the club. You were able to get him to admit it. If he brought her, maybe he brought in the rest?"

Peter had thought of this already. "We planted a girl for him, and he took the bait. He obviously didn't know her. But it does make me wonder if someone else was bringing these girls to the club, setting them up to meet József and be taken."

The director rubs his chin. "And who do you think that is?"

Peter shrugs. "The manager of the club, maybe."

"Didn't you say Zsuzsa knows him?"

Peter eyes Kovacs. They had agreed to keep Zsuzsa's role in the club between them. Peter supposes that secrecy doesn't extend to their boss. He nods at Kovacs.

"Who's Zsuzsa?"

"She's a bartender Peter knows. We planted her in the club on the weekends as part-time help. Just to see if she might come up with any useful information. We told her to keep her head down and not draw attention to herself. This was her first weekend in the club."

The director nods. "Well, maybe you can use her to locate that manager. What's his name?"

"Agoston," Peter and Kovacs say in unison.

Chapter 21

Renata

I open one eye as consciousness comes back to me. I'm still lying face down on the same mattress in the same room. I move my head to the side to open my other eye. Everything looks the same as before. The other girls are still across the room, asleep. *Why am I awake, and they aren't?* I push up on my elbow and examine the tube extending from my arm. There's a kink in it. A fold where whatever they've given me has stopped. That's probably why I woke up. Whatever is inside that bag isn't able to flow into my arm. I'm being drugged. My leg is still shackled to the bed frame, and I need this needle out of my arm.

A bandage is wrapped around my bicep, keeping the needle in. I hesitate to unwrap it, afraid of what I might find. I fight off the fear and unwrap it anyway. My skin is bruised around the spot of the needle. Besides an occasional shot, I've never had one inside me, and I wonder if this is normal. The needle is exposed now, and I can see it sticking into a vein. How am I going to take it out? *Should I pull it from the side? Maybe I just pull it up?* I worry about the implications of this. Will it bleed uncontrollably? I decide I have no choice and grab the spot where the needle connects to the tube and begin pulling. It reminds me of a time I was helping my father. We were fixing the stairs on our front porch. He gave me the hammer and had me pull nails from the old pieces of wood with the backside of the hammer. The needle was a nail, and my arm was an old piece of wood.

As the needle comes free, a pool of blood bubbles up from the hole. I hold my arm high and press my thumb against the bleeding gap. I sit, pressing my fingers to the crater, keeping my arm elevated. The pause gives me a chance to think. The last time I woke, I tried to free myself and, in the process, alerted my captor to my consciousness. I look down at the bed frame. They haven't fixed it. It's still loose. My leg remains shackled to it. There's enough play in the shackle to swing my leg off the bed. I move to the top of the bed and squeeze my slender frame between the headboard and wall. I push the bed frame away from the wall. A scraping noise erupts along the floor, sounding like a scratch on a chalkboard. I stop, shutting my eyes, cowering against the sound, hoping it wasn't as penetrating as I fear. At any moment, I expect to see that man reenter the room. But he doesn't. The only thing I hear is my own excited breathing. Last time, the banging headboard had brought him into the room. This time, I hope to push the bed out far enough that the headboard no longer reaches. I move back to the bed and begin to push and pull the frame back and forth. Before long, the screw comes loose, and I pull it from the headboard.

I slide my shackle to the end of the frame, and I'm free. I'm still shackled but no longer attached to the bed. The other end rubs against the wood floor as I walk. I move toward the door, conscious of every squeak the floor makes. I turn the handle and gently pull. I hear the sound of voices coming from down the hallway. The voices aren't present. They sound rehearsed. *Is it a TV or radio?* I take a breath working up the courage to look. Exhaling, I lean forward, looking down the hallway. It's coming from a TV. I can't see the screen, but note the shadows bouncing on the walls. At the end of the hallway is a door with an opening on both the right and left. The shadows and sound appear to be coming from the right.

I tiptoe to the end of the hall and stop in front of the opening. I stay crouched along the wall, listening—for what, I'm not sure. Probably any sign of the man. He must be around the corner, watching TV. But why can't I hear him? Why can't I feel his presence? The apartment feels empty. I dare to extend my head out toward the corner. Inching further and further. My left eye catches a glimpse of the room. There's a couch with a TV. The room is filthy. Beer cans, pizza boxes, and wrappers cover the floor. There's a couch, but it's empty. *Where is he?*

Just then, I hear the sound of footsteps behind me. They emanate from the kitchen across the hall. I step around the corner, and now I'm in the TV room, hugging the wall. The sound wasn't coming from the kitchen but from the other side of the front door. The doorknob turns, and I duck back behind the wall. My breathing is tight. Heavy feet enter the apartment, and I can't determine how many. The feet are so loud they might as well be a troop of soldiers. I'm stuck. If they come around the corner, I have nowhere to hide.

The room only has a couch and TV. I pray. *Please, God, let them go down the hall and away from me.*

They're in the kitchen now. Their voices are loud, but I can't make out any words. They sound angry. It sounds like they're arguing. They aren't speaking Hungarian. Something about that increases my fear. *If they aren't speaking Hungarian, what are they speaking?*

I hear one of them moving down the hall. He shouts, and the other joins him in the hallway. I silently kick myself. How could I have been so stupid as to leave the door to the room open? I risk it and poke my head around the corner just in time to see the second man enter the room. Now is my chance. I spring to the front door and throw it open. As I'm about to run down the hall, better sense comes to me. I quietly pull the door shut behind me. As I run through the hallway, I listen for noises behind me. I don't hear any yet, but I know I have seconds until I do.

I reach the stairwell to the apartment building; my surroundings are foreign. I take one step down the stairs and stop. Another thought flashes into my head. They don't know how long I've been gone. For all they know, I could have left the apartment right after they did. They'll come looking for me when they realize I'm not in the apartment. The first place they'll look will be down the stairs, then out on the street. I turn around and head back toward the apartment. But instead of going down the hall, I head upstairs. I have no idea what floor I'm on. I nearly trip as I rush up. Reaching the landing of the floor above, I hear heavy footsteps in the hallway below. The men realize I'm no longer in the apartment. They're on the stairs now, thundering downward, just as I had hoped. Within seconds I can no longer hear them. The stairway is silent, and I'm tempted to run to it and descend the stairs to freedom. I so badly want to be outside, away from them. But what if they're waiting for me on the stairs? What if they're waiting on the street just outside the apartment doors? I'm so completely alone.

I'm tempted to go back to the apartment. Free the other girls. Then I'd have some company. Others to help me. But what if the men come back? What if one of them never left the apartment? No, I'm going to stay here. My safest spot is waiting. I'll hunker down, wait for them to return, then sneak away.

Chapter 22

Detective Szabo

Look at him over there feeling so good about himself. He's only been here a few days, yet Kovacs is pulling him in to meet with the director. I've been here for ten years. It's supposed to be me. I started as a beat cop and had to work my way up to detective. When the task force formed, I was supposed to be Kovacs's right hand. I was the senior man. I know this city and country far better. This Peter shows up, and they act like he's God's gift to mankind. Well, I'm not going to take this lying down. I'm going to do something about it.

I stand and walk over to Detective Farkas. "Hey, come and join me in the small conference room for a few minutes." I look at Peter, making sure to keep my voice low. "And keep it on the down low. Just the three of us." I don't have to say who the three are. He knows.

Farkas looks up into my eyes. He's scrutinizing my face, waiting for more. Still, I give him nothing, and he eventually nods. I make my way over to Detective Varga, telling her the same thing. She agrees, almost like she's been expecting this. I ask her to wait a few minutes, trying to make it less noticeable.

I head over to the small conference room and sit down. After an appropriate amount of time, Farkas comes in.

"What's this about?" he asks.

I wave him away, telling him to wait until Varga gets here. After a couple more minutes, she slips in, closing the door behind her. When she's settled, I get right to it.

"Did you see how Kovacs pulled Peter in while talking with Toth?" I'm scowling as my eyes move from Farkas to Varga and back. "Any one of the three of us should have been in that meeting, not Peter. Kovacs is putting too much trust in him, and I don't like it."

They're looking at me, and I can tell they have the same concerns. They've seen it too.

"What do you want to do about it?" Varga asks.

I take a deep breath, almost like this is my first time considering it. "Well, first of all, the three of us have to agree to stick together. Share information among us. I think Kovacs and Peter are putting some things into play and aren't including the rest of us."

Varga frowns. "How do you know that? What are they putting into play?"

I shake my head. "Well, for one, did you know they have a bartender, a friend of Peter's, working in the club now?"

I could see the surprise register in Farkas's eyes. He clearly had no idea.

"Now, why wouldn't they tell us anything about that?" I wonder aloud.

Both of them are considering the implications. As a task force, we're supposed to share information among all five of us, but instead, they're holding secrets. Trust has been broken.

"How did you find out?" Varga asks.

"It doesn't matter; I just know. And from the looks on both of your faces, you didn't know about it either. Secondly, I don't trust Peter. It seems way too convenient that he just stumbled upon the human trafficking going on in the city. We know very little about him. He gets pulled into this task force. Why? Because he was a detective in New York? His wife was murdered, so he came back to Hungary? Now we have all this human trafficking going on? Hmm... Seems convenient that he's on the task force, doesn't it?"

Farkas shakes his head. "Wait, are you saying you think Peter might be dirty? Do you think he might be involved in the trafficking? They planted him here to keep an eye on the investigation?"

"Could be," I respond.

He looks doubtful, but when I look at Varga, she's nodding. "Maybe his wife found out something about him. They never solved the case, never found out who her murderer was. Maybe he had her killed?"

I hold up my hands. "Look, I don't know anything for sure. I'm just saying we need to be careful with him. The three of us need to work together and ensure we're all in the loop. For some reason, Kovacs is putting too much trust in him, and it's worrying me. I know the two of you are good cops. I can trust you."

They nod, and I feel better knowing we're all on the same page.

Chapter 23

Zsuzsa

Now I remember why I quit bartending in this club. It's three a.m., and I'm exhausted. Not only am I worn out, but I hurt. My feet ache, my back's tight, and my head won't stop ringing. *When did I become such an old lady?* It would be a blessing if I went the rest of my life without hearing techno music. I remember being younger, bartending in this same club. I didn't necessarily like the music, but I didn't hate it. Now I despise it. I can't take it. The constant thumping makes me queasy. If not for Peter, I'd walk out right now and never come back.

Oh… Peter. What is this hold you have over me? Why do I care so much about what you think? We had a lovely date a few weeks ago before the conversation turned to Andras. It wasn't just fun. It was the best date I've been on in years, maybe ever. I felt a connection with him. He's older but not too old. I felt so bad for him, what happened with his wife. I could feel his pain when he talked about her. Something about that made me want to hold him. When he kissed me, I wanted more. I haven't been kissed like that in a long time. He's such a good kisser.

But then he left to chase after Andras, and I didn't hear from him. I know he must have been going through a lot. He almost got killed and killed Andras in the process. But still, why couldn't he have called me? Wouldn't he have at least called if he really cared? Or at least wondered about me?

Now I'm here, working undercover *for him*. In an environment I hate. For what? I'm not even sure how much he cares for me. If I'm anything more than a friend. An acquaintance he once shared a drink with.

I look at Csaba, and he seems to be hitting a wall for the first time. Maybe that's just wishful thinking on my part. Hoping I'm not the only one who's barely able to stand. But he seems slower. Like he's lost the vigor he had earlier. There's finally a break in the constant drink requests, and he makes his way over.

"Hey, good job today. Thanks for your help. You did pretty well for your first time."

It's far from my first time, but I accept the compliment. I'm too tired to argue the point. The music stops, and the lights come on. I squint, waiting for my eyes to adjust to the light.

"I'll have Bela come to walk you out. I'm sure you're exhausted. I can handle the cleanup."

I consider arguing with him, but I'm too tired to feel anything but gratitude. I'm not entirely self-absorbed. I feel bad that he's staying to finish up alone. But he seems resigned to it. He sees my hesitation and convinces me it won't take him long, and he's used to it.

"Where's Agoston? I haven't seen him all night."

Csaba agrees. "Yeah, that's strange. I haven't seen him either. Normally he's front and center in the club. He must have got caught up in something."

I wonder what that *something* could be, but I don't say it.

"I wanted to thank him for the job again."

"Well, don't worry, you'll see him again. You can tell him next time."

Bela comes over, and Csaba tells him to walk me out. As we walk down the hallway toward the exit, he grabs me by the arm and pulls me back the other way.

"Hey, sorry, we aren't supposed to go this way. Let's go out the front," he tells me. I see what looks like panic on his face.

As we turn around and head back through the club, something has changed in him. He's agitated now. Almost like he's worried he's going to be in trouble. Like he's done something wrong. I know I shouldn't, but I can't help my curiosity. I'm supposed to keep quiet and just pay attention. Not ask questions.

"Bela, I haven't seen Agoston all night. Where is he?"

He turns and looks at me, and I can see he's trying to read why I'm asking. I smile back at him, trying to keep my look bright and innocent.

"I'm not sure. I saw him earlier but haven't seen him in a few hours."

His tone is wary. Is it because he doesn't like me asking because he thinks I'm testing him? Or because he doesn't want to be questioned?

We've reached the outside doors now, and I'm glad I'm wearing my thick coat. When the cold night air hits my lungs, it stings. I like Bela and don't want to see him lose his job. I decide I should warn him. If I noticed he's been stealing wine from the cellar, Agoston probably has.

"I hope he's not talking to the police. That wouldn't be good for you, would it?"

I'm surprised by the look he gives me. I'm expecting guilt, but that's not what I see in his eyes. I see anger.

"Why do you say that?"

His tone scares me. It's flat and cold. I shouldn't have said anything. Why did I open my big mouth? I decide to keep it cryptic. Let him think I don't know much.

"I just think you might be caught up in something illegal. And I don't want to see you in trouble."

His eyes narrow, then become sad.

"I hope you make it home safe, Zsuzsa. I liked working with you." His voice now sounds sorrowful, resigned.

"You too, Bela."

I begin to walk toward home. I hear nothing behind me, no door shutting, and I know he's still watching me. I can feel his eyes. I turn back around, and he's staring at me. I pick up my speed. I realize he said he liked working with me, past tense. What does that mean?

Chapter 24

Zsuzsa

That was weird. I can't figure Bela out. I see why he got angry when I implied he might be stealing from the club. He must be scared. He's probably worried I'm going to blow the whistle on him. I can't blame him; a guilty conscience has no peace. What I don't understand is, why did he look like he pitied me? Like he felt sorry for me?

My apartment is a five-minute streetcar ride from the club. But the streetcar isn't running this late, so I have to walk. It's not a long walk, normally twenty minutes. Ordinarily, I wouldn't mind so much; the snow has started to fall, and it's beautiful. But I can feel my face freezing. It's the only skin exposed to the chill. I wear an oversized coat with a hood covering my head. All I need is one of those locking facemasks, and I'd look like an old-time deep-sea diver. The streets are empty, unusual for a city of nearly two million people.

The night has gone from quiet to silent. The snow is falling harder now, muffling any noise. I can't even hear my own footsteps. What am I doing? It's three-thirty in the morning, and I'm walking through the snow heading home from a job I hate. Even if it's only temporary, I must be out of my mind. Peter shouldn't have asked me to do this. But even as I think it, I know it's not fair. He didn't ask me. I volunteered against his wishes. I'm the one who forced the issue, and made him consider it, got him to mention it to his boss. Even after his boss suggested I do it, he tried to talk me out of it.

So why am I walking home in the snow, freezing my face off? Is it really for Peter? I'd be lying if I didn't admit it's mostly about him. The chance to work with him and keep a connection. But it's more than that. I knew about Andras. I knew what he was. Okay... I didn't know *exactly* what he was. But I knew young girls at the restaurant were disappearing. When he'd threatened me, I knew that wherever they went wasn't by choice. I was scared, but I should have done something. How many of those girls could I have saved? I still see some of their faces in my head. They haunt me. This is my chance to help. Maybe clear my guilty conscience.

I cross the street, not bothering to look before I step off the curb. At this time of night, no need to worry about traffic. My foot slips as I step up to the other side of the street. I'm not wearing the best shoes for a stroll in the snow. I'm almost home. I can practically feel the warmth of my apartment. A hot shower, then climb into my bed. The pillow's softness and the duvet's warmth as I pull it up around me. I could sleep an entire day and night. Just one more block, and I'm there.

Around the corner, I see a dark figure step out onto the sidewalk. Even though he's at least fifty paces in front of me, I can see it's a man. He's tall. Even from here, his height is noticeable. He's coming toward me. He's looking down, but I see the orange glow of a cigarette as he sucks the warmth into his lungs. Although I don't smoke, tonight is a night where I get it. I can see the appeal of breathing in something warm. We're only ten paces apart. The distance is closing fast. Soon I'm close enough to smell the cigarette as he flicks it away. He still hasn't acknowledged me. I don't think he knows he's not alone. It's odd. He's coming right for me, but his head remains down. I step to the side to avoid running into him, but as I do, his head comes up, and he grabs me with one of his arms. He pulls me to him, turning me around. My back is to him, and I try to scream, but I can't. He holds a cloth in his hand, pressing it to my lips, muffling any sound. I take a deep breath, fighting to break free of him, but as I do, I smell something. Something sharp. I feel a pinch at my neck, and my mind begins to grow foggy. My legs give out. Before I go unconscious, I feel a surge of panic. They have me.

Chapter 25

Peter

Peter exits his apartment building Sunday morning. The sun is blinding. Even with closed eyelids, the light is penetrating. He holds his eyes shut for several seconds, letting his pupils adjust. When he finally opens his eyes, he does it slowly. It snowed overnight, but today the skies are clear. The sunshine radiates, reflecting off the snow. Peter loves days like today. Days where the snow has yet to be corrupted by dirt, maintaining its perfect whiteness. The scene is beautiful, but Peter wishes for sunglasses. He turns north on Váci Street and heads toward the streetcar stop. He's on his way to meet up with Zsuzsa. She worked last night in the club, and they had arranged to meet today so she could fill him in on anything she had learned.

Peter reaches the end of the block and looks left. The spot gives him a view of the Buda side of the city. The hills look enchanting, with a blanket of white nestled over the top. He notes the time looking down at his Breitling Chrono mat stainless-steel watch. Thirty minutes before he's due to meet her. Riding the streetcar will put him there too early. No point in sitting around waiting for her.

Deciding a walk in the crisp, clean air is a better alternative, Peter turns left and heads toward the river. Walking should get him to the coffee shop just in time.

As he makes his way along the icy sidewalk, he's careful about foot placement. His thoughts drift to his wife. Anytime he looks at his watch, he can't help remembering when she gave it to him on their tenth anniversary. He met Karen while working as a detective in New York City. She was robbed, and the thief had taken a valuable family heirloom. Peter had been entranced from the first time he had laid eyes on her. He made it his mission to get the jewelry back. Karen wanted to repay him when he did, and they settled on her cooking him a meal. Soon they were madly in love. They quickly married, and life was all he had ever dreamed it could be. He continued to work as a detective in the NYPD, and Karen as a nurse at Manhattan General.

Those ten years had been the happiest of his life. After spending a long day tracking down murderers or rapists, Peter could go home and take Karen in his arms. Seeing her eyes twinkle at him, hearing her laugh at one of his lame jokes, and feeling her lips on his sent jolts of electricity through his body. She was everything to him. He often thought he couldn't do his job without her in his life. Chasing bad guys just became too dark. It was too easy to allow the negative aspects of his career to cloud his overall view of humanity. But the light that was his wife balanced him out. She gave him perspective and kept him grounded. Not only did he love her, but he needed her. Without her, he wasn't whole.

As Peter reaches the river, he looks up to see the giant lion head statues that greet passengers of the Chain Bridge, the most iconic of the many bridges in Budapest. Named for the chains used to hold the roadbed in place, the Chain Bridge sits in the middle of the city, connecting the Buda and Pest sides. Peter loves to see the bridge at night, adorned with thousands of lights. But today, covered in newly fallen snow, the bridge looks as majestic as Peter can ever remember. Walking across the river, he notices large chunks of ice floating along. Miniature icebergs resembling those you might see in the oceans of Alaska or along the Norwegian coast.

Peter and Karen always wanted to visit Alaska. They had planned to take a cruise on their fifteenth anniversary. Peter's heart aches at the thought. That anniversary is only a few years away, and he'll be spending it alone. A year has passed since Karen's murder, but in some ways, the heartbreak is as fresh as ever. He left NYC to return to his home of Hungary, hoping it would help him move on. He shakes his head. No, that isn't it. He can never move on from Karen. Even the thought of that leaves him with a pang of guilt. No, it's more about memory. In New York, he could drive down a street or walk in the park, and memories of being there with her would flood back into his consciousness. The pain he felt seemed unbearable. In Budapest, he doesn't have any of those memories. Although they had talked about it, Peter never brought Karen to Hungary. Here, he isn't reminded of her on every corner.

He reaches the end of the bridge and turns right. He and Zsuzsa agreed to meet at eleven a.m. at Zërgë Coffeeshop. They picked Zërgë because of its central location. Zsuzsa lives in Buda. Peter lives

near the river in Pest. As he enters the coffee shop, he checks his
watch. Right on time. He looks around the shop, checking each
table. The shop is crowded, and it takes him a few minutes before
he's satisfied she hasn't arrived yet. Rather than order without her,
he'll wait.

He finds a table near the entrance, something that will allow him
a clear view of the front doors. As he sits people-watching, he tries
to push away the excited nervousness he feels. It reminds him of his
early dates with Karen. He can still remember sitting in the back of
that New York taxi on the way to her apartment, his leg bouncing
up and down. He couldn't figure out what to do with his hands.
His heart was pounding, and his stomach was turning. He thought
he might need to roll down the window and lose whatever was left
of his lunch. And it wasn't just because of the erratic driving of the
taxicab. When he finally arrived at her apartment and went upstairs,
he paused outside her door, straightened his clothes, brushed back
his hair, and checked his breath. He wanted her to see him as an attractive man, not just the detective who had recovered her property.
The friend zone was not the zone he wanted to be in.

When he finally did ring the bell, and she opened the door, her
smile lit a fire within him. He couldn't believe a creature that lovely
would smile at him. As he entered the apartment, he breathed in
the aroma of chicken parmesan. Karen was Italian-American. She
was taught how to cook by her mother, an Italian immigrant. As
good as the food smelled, it tasted even better. During the meal,
Karen's openness and sweetness showed through. She had gone all
out, making the meal memorable and attending to his every need.

At one point, early on, he made her laugh. He would never forget the angelic sound. From that moment on, it was his mission to hear it whenever they were together.

Peter hadn't felt like that with any other woman until Zsuzsa. When he first walked into Andras's bar and was served by Zsuzsa, he fell for her immediately. When she laughed, he was gone. It scared him.

Peter looks at his watch. Zsuzsa is twenty minutes late. He had only met her once for drinks, right after work. Maybe she's perpetually late. He sits anxiously checking his watch for another ten minutes. *Could she have forgotten?* After another ten minutes, his anxiety gives way to panic. *She isn't coming. Thirty minutes is too much.* Flashbacks of the night Karen never came home register in his mind. Did he do it again? Had a woman he loved been killed because of him? He has to move. He must find her and know she's safe. He rises from the table and heads out, looking for a taxi.

Chapter 26

Agnes

Today was my first day back at work, and I'm so glad it's over. Plastering a fake smile on my face as customers entered the shop was exhausting. Thinking of Renata, a couple of times, I broke down in tears. Once, about midway through my shift, a man walked in, and I thought it was Vik, the guy Renata and I had met in the club. His dark hair and athletic build highlighted the similarities. He reminded me so much of him that I could barely breathe. I stood there in a stupor, unsure which instinct would kick in, fight or flight. I knew it wasn't him when he finally looked up at me. I excused myself and went to the bathroom. I ran cold water into the sink, scooping it in my hands and splashing it on my face, trying to calm down. It was fifteen minutes before I could go back out there. Long enough for him to be gone.

Now I'm almost home. It's been five days since Renata was taken. My boss, the shop owner, after hearing what I had been through, let me have a few days off. Big of him, considering my best friend had been taken, and a man tried to abduct me. Today, his generosity ran out. He called me this morning demanding I return to work or find another job. I'm not surprised. All he seems to care about is money. My mind has been focused on cash also, but not for the same reasons. I can't help wondering what will happen to me if Renata doesn't return. *What if she's never found?* I can't afford this apartment on my own. I need money. I'm not going back home.

As I walk through my apartment door, I take a long look behind me. Today is the first day I've left home since returning from the hospital. All day I've felt eyes on me. Like someone is following me. This isn't me. I barely recognize myself. I was always the girl who jumped headfirst into trouble. Preferring to beg forgiveness rather than ask permission. Renata was the cautious one. She was my conscience, holding me back. Keeping me out of trouble. It doesn't feel real that she's gone. That she would be the one taken. *What happened? How could she put herself in that position? Why would she trust Vik?*

Shutting the door, I hear a crash in the kitchen. My heart leaps. He's back. He's come for me. He's in my apartment. I turn the knob to the front door, bracing myself to fly out, when Twain, our calico cat, slips around the corner and down the hall. Renata and I rescued him from the alley outside our apartment building a few weeks ago. I tiptoe toward the kitchen, hiding against the wall. I pause, listening. I hear nothing and peek my head around the corner. The bowl I'd left on the counter is lying on the linoleum floor. Twain knocked it off as he climbed on the counter. Not realizing I had been holding my breath, I exhale and take a few more. My heart rate returns to normal.

I enter the kitchen and bend down to pick up the bowl. I turn toward the sink, planning to place the bowl inside, when I hear a shrill buzzing sound coming from the hallway. I jump and lose grip on the bowl. It flies through the air and crashes on the porcelain sink splintering into a dozen pieces. The buzz sounds again, and I realize it's just the phone. I can't believe how jumpy I am. I leave the broken bowl and go to the ringing phone.

"Hello?"

"Agnes?"

I recognize the voice. It can't be.

"Renata," I nearly scream into the phone. "Is that you?"

"Agnes," she sobs into the other end.

Tears spring to my eyes. How could she be calling me? Where is she?

"It's me."

I can hear her crying.

"Where are you?"

"I don't know. I think I'm in Ukraine."

What? How? Why? That's a neighboring country but at least a ten-hour drive.

"I was taken outside the club. They drugged me. I escaped. They brought me here. I found a nice old lady on the street who took me in. I'm at her place now. She doesn't speak Hungarian. I don't know who I can trust."

My mind is spinning a mile a minute. I take a big breath, trying to calm down, but I can't help smiling. "The police know you were taken at the club. Let me call them. Do you have a number I can call you back on?"

I hear her hesitate.

"Do you know the address where you are?"

"I don't know anything. I don't know what to do."

She breaks down on the other end. It's no wonder, she's been through so much. My mind races. "Can you call me back in fifteen minutes?"

"I think so."

"I'm going to call the police. They'll know what to do." I look at the clock on the wall. "Call me back in fifteen minutes."

After hanging up, I rush back to my purse and fish out the paper Peter gave me. He wrote his number on it. I pick up the receiver and dial the digits. After six rings, I hear a pause, then Peter's voice. "This is Andrassy Peter. Please leave your phone number and name, and I'll call you back when I'm available."

Chapter 27

Peter

Peter hears his phone ringing as he inserts his key into the lock. After leaving the coffee shop, he went to Zsuzsa's apartment. He knocked on the door and rang the bell without an answer. Finally, losing all patience, he picked the lock and entered the apartment. The only thing he learned for sure was that she wasn't home. The apartment was clean and tidy, showing no signs of foul play. The bed was made, telling him nothing. Next, he tried to check with the neighbors on her floor, but they weren't home either. It wasn't until he went to the floor below that he found someone home—a grumpy, middle-aged couple said they knew Zsuzsa but hadn't seen her in a few days. He asked if they heard her come home last night. But they hadn't. Unfortunately, that information meant little. They said they rarely heard her. From their account, Zsuzsa is the perfect neighbor. The one everyone wants to live under.

He waited an hour outside her apartment, finally deciding to check Szépilona. Maybe Kata had heard from her. Not surprisingly, Kata hadn't seen her since her shift on Thursday night and didn't expect to see her until tomorrow. She said Zsuzsa, last they spoke, seemed perfectly fine, normal as ever. No indication she might be in trouble. Finally, he left, making Kata promise she would call the minute she heard from her. Now his phone is ringing, and his hopes soar. As he walks down the darkening hallway, the buzzing stops, and he hears his own voice. His answering machine has picked up. After asking the caller to leave a message, he hears a beep and grabs the receiver.

"Hello?" Peter asks. The voice on the other end is familiar, female. It isn't the voice he expects. She sounds out of breath with excitement. Almost like she can't wait for him to speak.

"Peter?"

"Agnes, what is it? What's wrong?"

"She's alive! Can you believe it? She's alive! She just called me."

Peter's thoughts were focused on Zsuzsa. How could Agnes know Zsuzsa is missing?

Without thinking, Peter asks, "Who's alive?"

"Renata. She just called me. She's alive."

He can barely comprehend what he's hearing. It's been almost a week since she was taken. He hadn't said it aloud to anyone, but he didn't think she would be seen again.

"Where is she?"

"She's in Ukraine. She's not sure where, exactly. She escaped. She's supposed to call me back in fifteen minutes. Can you come over?"

"I'll be right there."

Peter doesn't bother to knock as he reaches Agnes's apartment. Coming through the door, he finds her sitting at a small desk in the hallway. She's clutching the phone, speaking into it. Hearing him, she looks up, tears streaming down her face as she stands and holds the phone out to him.

He takes it from her. "Renata?"

"Yes?"

"This is Andrassy Peter. I'm a consultant with the Hungarian National Police here in Budapest."

The voice he hears on the other end is quiet and timid.

"Yes... Peter. Agnes told me who you are."

"Where are you?"

She hesitates. "I don't know. I was taken outside the Ötkert Club. I trusted the wrong guy."

"I know all about it. I know David lied to you. I know someone took you. But where are you now?"

"I don't know." Renata sobs. "I think I'm in Ukraine. The people don't speak Hungarian. It sounds like Russian, but I don't think it is. I took Russian in school."

She sounds like she's fraying at the edges.

He lowers his voice, speaking slowly and calmly. "It's okay. It's going to be all right. I'm going to find you. Let's work together to figure out where you are, okay?"

He hears her suck back her tears. After a few seconds, she says, "Okay."

"Good. Where are you now? Are you calling from a pay phone?"

"I escaped from my kidnappers. I was walking on the street, and a nice old lady saw me. She knew I needed help, but she doesn't speak Hungarian. She brought me to her house."

"Can I speak with her? Is she with you now?"

She calls out to the woman. After a few seconds, a new voice comes on the line.

"*Pryvit.*"

Peter knows almost no Ukrainian, but Ukrainian is a Slavic language, similar to Russian. He was forced to learn Russian as a kid growing up in Hungary during the Cold War, but that was many years ago, and he hasn't used it much since.

"*Privet, ty govorish' na angliyskom?*" *Hello, do you speak English?* he asks in Russian.

The woman rattles something back he can't quite understand, but he thinks he hears *nyet*, or *no*, somewhere in there.

"*Ya ne ponimayu.*" *I don't understand*, he tells her.

The woman slows her speech, nearly yelling into the phone. Enunciating each syllable. Again, Peter doesn't understand all of it, but he thinks he hears *vnuchka*, or granddaughter.

"Can I speak to your granddaughter?" he asks in what he hopes is recognizable Russian.

Again, she speaks slowly, and Peter recognizes the words *da*, yes, and *vnuchka*, granddaughter. It sounds like she'll allow him to talk with her granddaughter. The only question is if the girl is nearby. Peter sits on the phone waiting, and Renata comes back on.

"Peter?"

"Yes, I'm still here."

"I don't know what you said to her, but she just said something to me and left. She walked out the door."

He can hear the fear in Renata's voice. She understandably doesn't want to be left alone.

"It's okay. She left to get her granddaughter, who speaks English. I speak English also. Hopefully, then, we can communicate better."

Peter can hear the relief in Renata's voice.

"Okay, good."

While they wait, Peter decides to try and take her mind off being alone by asking her questions.

"Renata, are you okay? Are you hurt?"

Again, she begins to sob. "I'm scared. I don't know where I am. I don't know what they did to me, where they took me."

"I know. But listen. We're going to find you. I'll come for you as soon as I know where you are. I'll be there right away."

She cries harder now.

After a few seconds, she can speak again. "Thank you, Peter."

He can hear the murmur of voices in the background.

"She's back. I think this is her granddaughter."

"Put her granddaughter on the phone, will you?"

The next voice Peter hears is young; although she speaks English, it's heavily accented.

"Hello, this is Larysa."

"Larysa, this is Peter. Do you speak English?"

"Little bit."

Peter keeps his tone calm and slow, pronouncing every syllable. "My name is Peter. I am with the Hungarian National Police. That girl at your grandma's house is Renata. She is from Hungary. She has been kidnapped."

Peter stops speaking and waits. Hoping for a sign the girl might understand what he said.

"She was kidnapped?" the girl asks.

Peter has been holding his breath, and with her words, he exhales with relief. "Yes, she was kidnapped and escaped. Your grandma found her and brought her to the house. Where are you? Renata does not know where she is."

"We are in Kyiv in Ukraine."

After getting the address of the house, Peter asks the girl to translate for him. He tells her grandma who he is and who Renata is. The grandma promises to keep her safe until Peter arrives. He asks her not to take her to the police just yet. He isn't sure who he can trust. After that, he has the girl give the phone to Renata.

"Renata? Listen, I'll leave right away. I'll be there as soon as I can. They know who you are and have promised to keep you safe until I arrive. I'll see you soon. Okay?"

As Peter hangs up, he looks at Agnes. Before he can say anything, she's excitedly talking.

"I just need to pack a bag. I'll be ready in five minutes."

Peter frowns. "What? You aren't coming with me."

Agnes turns back, putting a hand on her hip. "Oh yes, I am."

"Oh no, you're not. Someone tried to take you just a few days ago. We don't even know who we can trust in Ukraine. We don't know who might be working with these guys. It's better if I just go and get her."

Peter can see the heat rising in her cheeks.

"My best friend, the one I convinced to go to that club, the one I convinced to move to Budapest with me, was taken a few days ago. She just called me. But you don't think I should go? I'm going. Even if I have to follow you to the train station and jump on. Besides, you won't be here to protect me. They tried to get me here also. Remember?"

He has to acknowledge there's logic to this. Renata hasn't met Peter and would undoubtedly feel more comfortable and safer if Agnes were with him. But they don't know who the bad guys are there. They wouldn't know them if they sat beside them on the train. Peter begins to shake his head again, but Agnes's eyes fill with tears.

"Peter, it's my fault she's gone. Let me start to make it up to her."

In spite of himself, he can't say no to a crying girl.

Chapter 28

Peter

Peter exhales as he takes his seat in the second-class cabin of the train. After leaving Agnes's apartment, they stopped by Peter's so he could get a bag. He almost skipped it, feeling pressure to make the train station and find the schedule. He would never forgive himself if he missed a train heading to Ukraine by only minutes. But as they arrived and checked the schedule, they found a train from Budapest to Kyiv leaving within the hour. They purchased tickets and now sat on the train heading east.

"I still can't believe it," Agnes tells Peter. "She's alive. And she's okay."

That's a severe overstatement, but Peter can see why Agnes would say it, given her age. Experience had taught him what abductions could do to a person. To say she's okay was naïve, at best. He worries about what could be waiting for them in Kyiv. Even if Renata looks the same on the outside, he knows this experience has changed her and likely the girls' relationship.

"It's great news, for sure," Peter acknowledges.

After several minutes of silence, Agnes looks at him, raising an eyebrow. "There's been something I've been wondering about. Something you said to Renata when you were talking to her on the phone."

Peter knows where this is going but waits for the question.

"You said she was taken by a guy outside the club. That she was brought to him by David." Agnes shakes her head. "The man we met in the club was named Vik, not David."

"Is there a question in that?" Peter asks, raising an eyebrow back at her.

A little flustered by his response, Agnes rolls her eyes. "Who's David?"

This is a conversation Peter would rather not have. Since reading about David in Renata's journal, he knew Renata was keeping her relationship with him from Agnes. What he didn't know was why. He also doesn't want to be the one to disclose information about Renata that she clearly doesn't want Agnes to have.

"Was Vik actually David?" Agnes watches him closely. "Did she know him before going to the club?" As she asks these questions, her eyes widen with understanding. Peter decides saying nothing is his best path, letting her come to her own conclusions. "Had they planned to meet there? Was Renata dating him?"

Peter stares back at her, remaining silent. Realization, then betrayal, flash across Agnes's face. Seeing he isn't going to say anything, she turns away, looking out the train window. "Why wouldn't she just tell me?" she says in a whisper, no longer speaking to Peter. "What else was she keeping from me?"

Peter feels for her. Learning someone has been lying to you, or at least keeping things from you, hurts. But your best friend? The girl you grew up with? That kind of betrayal is devastating for a girl her age.

"Agnes," Peter says, pulling her back from her thoughts, "why did you and Renata come to Budapest?"

Agnes looks at him, frowning. She's in another place, and this question confuses her. Staring back at him, he sees her eyes come into focus. She's tracking with him now. "We had always wanted to come. After school was over, we decided to."

Having read Renata's diary, Peter knows this isn't the whole story. "You both wanted to come? Or you wanted to come, and Renata did it for you?"

Agnes frowns back at him. "Wait, what?"

Peter inclines his head, looking at her. "You know what I'm talking about."

She gives him a look, but as he holds her gaze, she squirms.

"Okay, it was mostly me. Neither of us did very well on our final examinations. Renata wanted to become an engineer, and I wanted to be a microbiologist. After we got the results, neither of us had those options anymore. At least, we wouldn't have been able to qualify for the schools in Budapest. That's when we decided to come up to Budapest anyway."

Peter knows part of this is true; Agnes hadn't done well on her exams, but Renata had. In fact, she did so well, she could have easily gotten into the school she wanted. She kept that from Agnes, sparing her feelings. She had enrolled in the school unbeknownst to

Agnes. Peter couldn't understand why they had come as quickly as they had, basically running away from home after school got out. School for Renata wouldn't start until September.

"You weren't running away from anything?" Peter asks.

She can't hold his gaze and again looks out the window. Peter is surprised to see tears form in Agnes's eyes. After a minute, she says, "There was this boy, Dominick, that we grew up with. We've known him since we were little. We all went to school together. All the girls loved him. He was the best football player in the school, so athletic. He was smart and confident. He had dark-brown hair and piercing, gray eyes."

She looks down and rubs her thighs. "Both Renata and I loved him. All the girls did. Most wouldn't even talk to him because he was so intimidating. But I always did. I'm about the only girl in the school that he did talk to. He was shy, but most girls thought he was cocky. Anyway, it made me think he liked me. I thought it showed there might be something between us because he only talked to me. He'd even come over to my house sometimes. He's in Budapest now also, playing on a football team."

She waves her hand dismissively. "On the last day of school, I got my exam results. They were terrible, and I was upset. The only thing that made it even somewhat okay was that I would be able to dance with Dominick that night." She stops and looks at Peter. "On the last day of school, it's tradition to hold a dance. In the past years, Dominick never danced with any of the girls. Only me. Mostly because I would ask him. He didn't ask me."

A tear rolls down her cheek, and she reaches up and rubs it away with the palm of her hand. "Well, Dominick wasn't dancing at the dance, like always. I walked over and asked him to dance." She looks out the window, and her voice gets softer, almost like a whisper. Peter leans forward so he can hear her. "While we were dancing, I decided to tell him how I felt about him. How I had loved him since we were five years old. I hoped he would tell me he loved me too. That he was so glad I told him. I dreamed of him kissing me right there on the dance floor."

She looks up into Peter's eyes, tears brimming. "Just as I was about to tell him, he asked me about Renata. About what she was going to do after school. Where she was going to go. I didn't think too much of it and asked him why he cared." A sob escapes her throat, and she puts her hand over her mouth, trying to silence her cry. She looks back out the window. Her face crumpling in pain. After a moment, she gains control and turns back to him. "That's when he told me how he felt about her. How he had always liked her but never felt courageous enough to approach her."

Agnes shakes her head and folds her hands in her lap. "I was crushed. I felt like everything I wanted was gone that same day. After the dance, I ran out of school. Renata chased after me. She wanted to know why I was so upset, but I couldn't bring myself to tell her everything. I told her about my exam scores but never told her about Dominick. She told me she hadn't done as well as she had hoped. That's when we came up with a plan to leave home and come to Budapest. We left the next morning. Never saying goodbye."

Tears stream down her face, and several passengers steal glances in her direction. Most probably assume Peter and Agnes are father and daughter. Peter looks down, trying to give her as much privacy as possible. Agnes stands and excuses herself to head to the restroom.

Peter sits pondering how Renata might feel knowing the boy she had grown up loving, liked her back, and her best friend kept it from her. For being best friends, these girls had some trust issues between them.

Chapter 29

Peter

Peter sits looking out the train window. Across from him, Agnes has curled her legs under her, leaning against the wall, asleep. It amazes him how quickly she can nod off, given all that's happening. Although, who can blame her? In the last few days, she's experienced the shock of losing her best friend, nearly being abducted herself, then learning the best friend is alive. Who wouldn't be exhausted from the emotional rollercoaster that would cause? Looking at her, he thinks back to when he was an eighteen-year-old. *Kid* is the correct term. Eighteen is only an adult according to the government and the person with the birthday. At sixteen, he left home. No, he had been *kicked out* of his home. His father had never understood him, and friction abounded. Without warning, he found himself homeless. That night he left his hometown of Pécs and jumped a train to Budapest. Budapest hadn't abounded with opportunity like he had hoped. After only a few weeks working in a factory, he snuck out of Hungary, crossing the border to Austria.

Post-WWII, America was experiencing a boom in manufacturing and commerce. He was able to get a visa to America to begin a new life. He arrived in New York City full of wonder. For a kid who grew up in Pécs, Budapest had been huge. New York City felt like a different planet. He couldn't get over the size of the buildings, let alone the number of people. Lying about his age, he found work in a steel-manufacturing plant. He knew almost no English and was utterly alone. He shared an apartment with two other factory workers, neither from Hungary. He had no choice but to grow up fast.

Sitting across the row from Agnes, he couldn't help but feel their common bond. Like Agnes, he had been forced from home and went to Budapest. Like Agnes, he had been hurt and wounded by someone he loved and had wanted to put as much distance between himself and them as possible. He felt a strong desire to protect her and Renata. To help them just as he had been helped in New York City so many years ago.

That wasn't all that was occupying his thoughts. Zsuzsa had disappeared, and he knew who had taken her. Something happened at the club, and they learned why she was there. Peter knew from his experience with Andras that when a woman is abducted, they move her. Andras was moving the women to Croatia; the club is moving them to Ukraine. He knows his window to save Zsuzsa is small, and he can't hesitate, or she'll be gone. When he learned Renata was in Ukraine, he knew Zsuzsa likely was also if she was still alive.

He feels a shift under the train and knows the brakes have been engaged. They begin to slow down. Looking out the window, he sees the city sign for Nyíregyháza. He's never been to the city but knows it's the final station before crossing the Ukrainian border. Knowing the border patrol will soon arrive, he stands and pulls down his suitcase. The movement wakes Agnes, and she looks up at him.

"Are we here?"

Peter shakes his head. "No, we're still in Hungary. We're coming into Nyíregyháza. They'll be checking our passports."

Looking confused, she asks, "What's a passport?"

Peter looks at her sharply. "You don't have a passport?"

She shakes her head. "No, I didn't know."

Peter exhales and begins to chew the side of his mouth. He knows he should have checked with her earlier. This is a girl who grew up in the country. She's likely never left Hungary. Budapest was as far as she imagined going. It makes sense she wouldn't think of a passport. *What do I do?* He looks out the window and sees they haven't reached the train station. His mind races, considering his options.

Finally, he looks down at Agnes. "Grab your bag, and follow me. Say nothing, even if someone stops you."

He had noticed a small baggage room across from the bathroom when they entered the train. Maybe he'd be able to hide her in there. She's small, perhaps only a hundred and ten pounds, and just over five feet. Train passengers begin to fill the hallway, waiting to disembark. They would have to do the same or look like they were. He would stash her in the baggage room when the time was right.

The train comes to a stop, and people begin to file off.

Peter leans down to whisper in Agnes's ear. "There's a luggage room across from the bathrooms. I need you to get there before people come back on the train. Find a spot to hide. Stay out of sight. Go now."

Peter walks to the car entrance, blocking the way as people begin to try and climb on board. Ten people stand at the bottom of the stairs waiting. The first person, a woman, asks Peter to step aside. He ignores her, pretending not to hear her. Seeing she's not being listened to, she yells up at him. Peter goes on ignoring her, blocking the way. He has to give Agnes plenty of time to stow her suitcase and find a hiding spot in the extra luggage room. Finally, a train conductor comes by, hearing the ruckus and seeing the mass of people not boarding the train. He moves past the woman, stepping up to Peter.

"Sir? Will you move, please?"

Peter keeps his back to the man, pretending not to hear him. The conductor taps Peter on the shoulder. Knowing he can't delay any longer, Peter turns and gazes at him, a bewildered look on his face. The train conductor motions to the people standing behind him.

"Please move. These people are trying to get on the train."

Peter cups his hand to his ear, leaning forward. "What was that?"

The train conductor exhales. In a much louder voice, he yells, "Move back. These people want on the train."

Peter feels like his head might explode from the man yelling in his ear, but he tries not to show it. He looks up, pretending to see the angry mob for the first time. He holds up his hands. "Oh, I'm sorry." He steps back, heads toward the bathroom, and leans against the wall. As people file on the train, many mutter obscenities toward him. Peter has to fight not to laugh when one woman implies his mother made a mistake when she decided to have sex with his father.

Once they all pass, he opens the luggage room. Agnes has done an excellent job. He can't see her anywhere.

"Agnes?" he whispers.

He hears a muffled response from the back corner behind several pieces of luggage.

"Good job. Stay put until I come to get you."

Peter shuts the door and walks back to his seat. Within five minutes, the border patrol comes by checking passports. Peter holds his out to the man. The official takes it from him, eyeing it curiously. United States passports are a rarity on a passenger train from Hungary to Ukraine. After checking it closely, he stamps it and hands it back to Peter.

As the man moves on, Peter sits anxiously, looking down the hallway toward the luggage room. Two men are checking passports. One walks right past, but the other stops and opens the door. Peter's fears are realized when the man steps inside. Peter stands and walks down the hallway. He stops and listens outside the room. He can hear the man moving luggage around. He's going to find Agnes. Peter knocks on the door and steps inside. The officer looks up, surprised to see Peter.

"Sir, do you speak Hungarian?" Peter asks in Hungarian.

The man furrows his brow. "Of course."

Peter exaggerates relief. "Oh, good. I need some help."

The man is bent over, moving bags around, and stands. He walks out the door, following Peter. Peter turns back to him in the hallway.

"Can you tell me how many more stops there will be until we arrive in Kyiv?"

The man gives Peter an exasperated look, then turns his head toward the ceiling and begins to tick off his fingers as he counts the stops. "I think about eight."

"Thank you."

The man nods and turns back to head inside the luggage room, giving Peter a look like, "That was it? That was the emergency?" Peter hoped the distraction would be enough for the man to move on, saving Agnes. Not so lucky. Before the man reenters, Peter grabs his arm. The man looks down at Peter's hand, then glares up at him.

"Sir." Peter holds out some Ukrainian Hryvnia. It's a risk but a calculated one. He's guessing most of the border patrol can be bought, but how much will it take?

The man looks at the money, then back up at Peter. "What's this for?"

Peter smiles. "You seem like a busy man. You probably don't get paid enough for all the work you have to do. I'd like to help you out and give you this money in payment for not finishing your search of the luggage room."

The man eyes Peter. "Thank you, but I really need to look through everything."

Peter feels the disappointment like a punch to the gut.

"But, I guess I could move on if that money was double."

Peter feels relief. But he knows this isn't over. He gambles again. "Sorry, this is all I have." He holds it up to the man, encouraging him to take it.

The man eyes Peter, then looks up and down the hallway. He reaches out and takes the money, stuffing it in his coat. He tips his hat to Peter. "Enjoy your time in Kyiv."

Peter smiles and heads back to his seat. Agnes will need to stay in the luggage room for a while yet, but it looks like they've avoided a catastrophe for now.

Chapter 30

Peter

Peter feels his anxiety rise as the shudder of brakes indicates they're arriving in Kyiv, a city he's never been to. Actually, he's never been east of Hungary. Although he grew up in Hungary, then a part of the Soviet Union, he had lived most of his life in America. The United States in the '60s, '70s, and '80s, saw Russia as the enemy. Peter believed that more than most Americans, having grown up in a Soviet state. He saw firsthand the adverse effects of communism. The difference between West and East was evident when he arrived in New York City. Technology, healthcare, education, and quality of life were all better in the West. The first time he had ever seen an orange was in NYC.

A pang of guilt hits him as he looks at the girl sitting across from him. Should she be here? Maybe he was wrong to bring her. This is a country he's unfamiliar with. In his mind, the closer you get to Russia, the more you can't trust the government or police. How is he going to keep her safe?

He knows he can't let any of these concerns show. Agnes will be scared already; she'll be relying on him. In the Budapest train station, he picked up a map of Kyiv. During the long train ride, he spent hours studying it. Now, he feels more confident about his knowledge of the city. But he knows looking at a map and traveling in a city are two different things. They would be coming into Pasazhyrski train station, the largest in Kyiv. From there, they would need to somehow get to Thirty-One Serhiia Paradzhanova.

Heads bob as the train stops. People rise from their seats and scurry toward the exit.

Agnes turns to him. "Where do we go?"

Peter smiles. "To an address I can't pronounce. Come on, get your bag. Let's get off this train and figure it out."

It's been a few hours since he's stood to stretch his legs. He feels the tightness of his muscles and joints as he moves. It's taken an entire day to travel the 693 miles, and he can't wait to get some fresh air, even if it's frigid. After descending the stairs, they follow the mass of people toward the exit doors. Peter's been to many train stations, and this one doesn't feel much different. As they exit, the wind bites through their clothing. Hungary gets cold in the winter, but this feels worse.

Peter scans the horizon getting his bearings. A busy street runs in front of the train station and, beyond that, a bus stop. Further away, he can see tall buildings indicating the city center. A row of white cars with yellow trim sits between the busy street and the bus stop. Each has a number assigned. Those must be taxis. He turns to look at Agnes. Her nose and cheeks are already turning red from the cold.

"Moment of truth now," he tells her.

"What do you mean?"

"Let's see if any of these taxis can communicate with us enough to take us to Renata." He motions with his head for her to follow. The admonition was unnecessary; she hadn't let him out of arm's length since stepping off the train. Now she's glued to him.

He walks up to the first taxi choosing to speak English. The further you get from Hungary, the lower the chance someone speaks it, let alone recognizes it. Even in Eastern Europe, English is becoming increasingly popular.

"Do you speak English?" he asks the driver as he rolls down his window.

The man looks at him, says something in Ukrainian, and shakes his head. Peter is about to turn away when the driver holds up a finger, climbing out of the car. As he stands, he keeps his finger extended, indicating they should wait. He runs forward two cars and leans over to the driver's side window, speaking to another taxi driver. The other taxi driver returns to where Peter and Agnes are standing.

Extending his hand to Peter, he says with a heavy accent, "Hello, I am Oleg. Nice to meet you."

Peter smiles, taking his hand. "Hi, Oleg. I'm Peter, and this is Agnes."

Oleg shakes Peter's hand, then extends his hand to Agnes. Agnes takes it, and Oleg tells her it's nice to meet her. She says nothing and looks back at Peter.

"She doesn't speak much English," Peter explains.

Oleg withdraws his hand, trying again in Ukrainian. Agnes shakes her head, leaning into Peter.

"She doesn't speak Ukrainian either."

Oleg looks surprised but shrugs, looking back at Peter.

"Oleg, can you take us to this address?" Peter fishes a paper from his pocket and shows it to him.

Oleg takes the paper and examines it. "Of course. My car is here." He points back to the taxi. He reaches out for Peter's bag. Peter gives it to him, but when he reaches for Agnes's, she steps away, not letting him touch her bag. Oleg gives her a curious look and puts his hands up but turns and starts walking toward his car, motioning for them to follow. Peter and Agnes fall in behind him. As they reach the car, Peter opens the door to the back seat and slides in. Agnes joins him, and Oleg shuts the door.

While Oleg walks around to the front, Peter whispers to her, "Don't speak any Hungarian. Just remain silent and let me do the talking." Agnes looks at him and nods, clutching her bag. Peter knows he's probably worrying too much, but he can't be too sure. If Renata's captors had brought her here, there must be a network in Kyiv. Oleg opens the driver's side door and slides behind the wheel, proclaiming, "Okay, we go."

Oleg pulls out and drives a few blocks before speaking to Peter again.

"You are English?"

Peter shakes his head. "No, I'm from America. New York City."

Oleg turns around in his seat, no longer keeping his eyes on the road. It reminds Peter of the opening scenes of *Dumb and Dumber* when Jim Carry drives Lauren Holly to the airport. Multiple accidents result, and he hopes the same won't happen here.

"New York? Empire State Building. Statue of Liberty."

Peter nods, praying Oleg will turn back around. "Yes. That's New York."

Oleg finally turns back, but he's watching Peter in the rearview mirror, paying almost no attention to the road. "Why are you in Kyiv?"

"I came to visit a friend. Someone I knew from New York who lives here."

The car in front of them slams on its brakes, and Oleg looks down just in time. After yelling something in Ukrainian, he looks back at Peter. He turns the wheel, and Peter sees his eyes dart toward Agnes. "And the girl?"

Peter shrugs. "She doesn't hear well." He points to his ears. "She has a hard time talking."

Oleg nods. "Welcome to Kyiv. I hope you enjoy your time."

For the next ten minutes, Oleg drives while Peter and Agnes remain silent, looking at their new surroundings. The city doesn't seem wildly different from Hungary. The most significant difference is the writing. Ukraine, like Russia, uses the Cyrillic alphabet. Oleg turns the car, and they enter a residential street. The houses are old, probably built in the 1950s or '60s.

After driving through the neighborhood, Oleg pulls in front of a green house and parks.

"This is house."

Peter thanks him and motions for Agnes to get out. He has no idea how much Ukrainian Hryvnia to give him. "How much?"

Oleg hesitates, and Peter wonders if it's because he wants to see how much Peter has.

"I don't know how you say."

Peter nods and shows Oleg some, not all, of his money. Oleg points at one of the bills saying, "it's okay." Peter hands him the bill, and Oleg thanks him.

"My bag is in the trunk," Peter tells him.

"Oh, yes." He opens the driver's side door and rushes to the back. He pops the trunk and gives Peter his bag. Peter and Agnes wave goodbye to Oleg and walk to the gate.

The lot is surrounded by a fence, including a bell that rings into the house. Peter steps up, pressing the bell. They hear a buzzing inside the house. After several seconds an older woman with black hair and bright lipstick comes to the door. She looks at Peter and Agnes, confusion on her face. They don't look like anyone she's expecting. The grandmotherly woman takes a few steps out of the house and rattles off something to them in Ukrainian. Peter answers in Russian. As soon as she hears it, she recognizes his voice. She rushes down the stairs and path to the front gate throwing it open. She opens her arms wide, a large smile on her face. Peter hesitates, but she rushes him and throws her arms around him. She motions for them to come in. Peter turns and waves to Oleg, and he pulls away.

The friendly woman continues to yammer on in Ukrainian, waving her arm in a motion for them to follow. Two cats come out of the house, and she yells at them, shooing them back inside. As they enter the house, Peter looks to his left and sees a girl sitting on the couch. She looks exhausted and frightened, but he recognizes her immediately. Behind him, he hears a scream, and Agnes pushes past him. Renata, having seen Agnes, yells and jumps to her feet. They meet in the middle of the floor, squeezing each other, laughing, and crying. The childhood best friends are together again.

Peter sits at the kitchen table, listening to the girls in the other room. They've been separated for a week, but they act like it's been fifty. In a way, it makes sense. They have been together almost every day since being five years old. They're used to always being together. Now, they sit on the couch, holding each other as cats crawl over and around them. He's lost count of the times Agnes tells Renata, "I thought I'd never see you again."

As he watches them, he takes a moment to look around the house. It's not large but nicely decorated. The walls are adorned with family photos and landscape paintings. Peter stands and walks into the room, watching the girls. Looking at Renata, he's pleased to see her demeanor has brightened. When they first walked in, a dark cloud surrounded her. He feared she would never recover from the last week. Seeing her now, he feels some hope. Not long after arriving, the kind older woman left to get her granddaughter, leaving them alone in her house. Peter decides it's time to talk with Renata. He moves to stand in front of the girls.

"Renata, it's so good to see you. I'm Peter. We talked on the phone."

Renata smiles, tears still trickling down her face. "Yes, I assumed. Thank you for coming for me."

"My pleasure. We're going to get you back home as soon as we can. But I need to ask you a few questions. Is that okay? I don't want to push you, but there are things I need to know."

Renata gives him a wary look. "I don't remember much. I probably won't be of help."

Peter nods. "That's okay. Whatever you can tell me will be a big help. Do you remember where they held you? Could you get back there?"

Renata's face goes white with fright. "I don't want to go back there. Please, don't make me go back." She begins to cry, and Agnes wraps her in a huge hug patting her back and glaring at Peter.

"No... no, Peter won't take you back. He's only asking if you know where it is."

Renata continues crying, and Peter sits in the rocking chair opposite the couch. This hasn't started well.

After a few seconds, Renata gets a hold of her emotions and shakes her head. "I don't know. That was really scary. I was focused on getting out. The drugs they gave me made my head cloudy. I couldn't focus. I'm sorry."

"No need to apologize. Did you say other girls were there?"

Renata looks at him with red, puffy eyes. "Yes, there were three others."

Peter's mind flashes to Zsuzsa. *Would they take her there?*

Shuffling feet can be heard at the front of the house, then the door opens. The old woman is back, followed by a petite teen blond girl. The old woman sees Peter sitting in the rocking chair. She motions to her granddaughter, saying something about Peter and pointing. The grandmother sits on the couch and picks up a cat. She begins petting it while repeating the word *Ragnar*.

Peter stands and waves to the girl. "Larysa?"

The girl smiles, but the grandmother is doing the talking, all in Ukrainian. The girl smiles and puts her finger to her grandmother's lips. She turns back to Peter and shakes her head while patting the woman on the shoulder. The older lady looks at Peter and blushes. She says something else in Ukrainian, then clamps her hand over her mouth. Peter smiles and waves her away, telling her it's no problem. The old woman keeps her mouth shut but motions to her granddaughter to talk with Peter. The love is evident between them as they smile at each other.

The girl approaches Peter. "Yes, Peter, I Larysa," she says in English.

"Great. I kind of assumed."

Larysa laughs. "My grandmom is not used to foreign people."

"No need to explain. We are so grateful to her for helping Renata."

Larysa grins as she looks over to Renata and Agnes.

"Will you ask your grandmother something for me?"

Larysa looks back at him. "Of course."

"Can you ask her if she can take me back to where she found Renata?"

"Yes."

Larysa turns to her grandmother, rattling something in Ukrainian. When the older woman responds, Peter doesn't understand what she says, but he can see her head bobbing. He breathes a sigh of relief. Between her and Renata, he feels hopeful he can find Zsuzsa.

Chapter 31

Detective Kovacs

I feel my eyebrows lower as I look out from my office into the bullpen. *Where is he?* I put my neck on the line with the director. It was my suggestion we add him to the team. He's making me look bad. He's late. The rest of the group is here. Szabo is going to have a field day with this. *Where is he?* We have our weekly briefing in thirty minutes, and he's nowhere to be found.

I look down at the forms on my desk. I need to concentrate. I can't worry about Peter; I need to get these done. For the next ten minutes, I mindlessly move papers around. My thoughts are elsewhere. Finally, I've had enough. I grab the phone on my desk and dial his number. After several rings, his answering machine picks up. My frustration is boiling over, evident from the message I leave. I let loose on him when I hear the beep: "Peter, where are you? We have a meeting with the director in twenty minutes. You know that. Today is not the day to be late. You better be on your way and have a good excuse for not being here. I'm beginning to doubt my decision to bring you on. Get here now!"

I slam down the phone, and a few heads turn in my direction, having heard me through the open door. I make eye contact with Szabo and see the smirk on his face. *What's with him? What does he have against Peter?* My eyes drop back down to the forms, but then I hear the booming voice of the director. He's greeting people as he walks into the bullpen. He stops and talks with Szabo. I can't hear what they say, but I can tell from their body language they're having a good time. After a minute, he throws back his head in laughter. He slaps Szabo on the shoulder, pointing at him as he walks away. He's coming to my office.

I stand as he enters. His smile vanishes as he looks at me. He closes the door, shutting out the rest of the team. He commands me to sit back down while he takes one of the chairs across the desk. He never does this. *Why is he here? Has he noticed Peter is missing?*

"I got a call this morning. You have some explaining to do."

His face is impassive. I feel a bead of sweat trickle down my back.

"Has one of your agents gone rogue? Or did you tell him to do it?"

I have no idea what he's talking about, but I don't want him to think I can't handle my position. I don't see any advantage to speaking at this point, and stare back at him.

"Why is Peter crossing the border into Ukraine?"

He's watching me closely, but I do my best not to react. I'm shocked. *Ukraine?* I have no answer for him, but I don't want him to know. I take a chance. "He's following up on a lead we had from there."

"What lead?"

My mind is scrambling. "David... or József, you know, the guy we got in the club. He told us the girls are being sent to Ukraine, not Croatia."

Surprise registers on the face of the director, and he leans back in his chair. "You never told me this before? I thought he didn't know anything about where the girls go after he drops them in the alley?" He glowers at me. This is not the kind of man you want angry with you. The expression "if looks could kill" was invented because of him. Once, a few years ago, he went through three secretaries in a month. Two of them left crying and were too afraid to return and get their final paychecks. They had to be mailed.

"He just told us that. I learned it yesterday. I haven't seen you since. I planned to tell you in our meeting today. He had said nothing about it in our first interview."

The director's expression is unchanged. He stands and leans across the desk, pointing a finger at my chest. "I've told you this before. I'll be told whenever you have new leads on this trafficking ring. No matter what time of day. Especially when it means one of our agents is leaving the country." He slows his voice. "This had better not happen again. I don't appreciate being made a fool when I get a call about something I'm completely unaware of. I know everything. No matter what. Do you understand me?"

I swallow hard, my Adam's apple bouncing up and down. "Absolutely, sir. It will never happen again."

He straightens, making his way to my office door. I realize I'm holding my breath, and I'm getting lightheaded. Before he opens the door, he turns back to me. "The meeting this morning is canceled.

Something else has come up. In lieu of the meeting, I want you to write a report. I want a full rundown of where we stand. I want to know all new information and a full description of each team member's workload. And it had better be on my desk by noon."

He stares into my eyes, and I don't trust myself to speak. I nod, and he spins on his heel, opening the door. As he walks through the bullpen, he says something to Farkas, smiling, and Farkas laughs. Just as quickly as he came, he's gone. I sit back in my chair, placing my hand on my forehead and wiping away the sweat. *What is Peter doing to me? Why would he leave for Ukraine and not tell me?* Something must have happened. *But what?*

Then it hits me. *Zsuzsa!* Only one thing would make him leave Budapest and go to Ukraine. Something must have happened to her. I nearly knock a folder off my desk as I stand. Grabbing my jacket, I rush out into the bullpen. I call for everyone's attention and tell them the staff meeting has been canceled. Without explanation, I head toward the exterior doors. I have no idea where Peter is going and have no way to contact him. I need to find out what he's learned, and I'm not going to know by sitting in the office preparing a report.

Twenty minutes later, I enter the club. There isn't anything subtle about my arrival. I've been here before. The last time I came, I remained conspicuous, never drawing attention to myself. I selected a booth in a dark corner. Somewhere I could keep an eye on the dance floor. I ordered a couple drinks, barely touching them. This time I want them to know who I am. I flash my badge at the bouncer standing guard at the front door. I demand he lets me inside. Surprised, he provides little resistance as I walk past him. Behind me, I hear him on the radio. Probably alerting his boss to my presence. It's late morning on a Monday, and the club resembles a funeral home rather than one of the most popular hangouts in town. Besides the bouncers, the only people I see are cleaners trying to remove all evidence of a wild weekend.

I marvel at how plain this place looks with the lights on. For one, it's not nearly as big as I thought. It's also somewhat drab, void of decorations or interior design. I stop and look around as I reach the center of the dance floor. A man rushes down the stairway toward me. He looks like he can't decide whether he should greet me or run in the other direction.

"Sir, can I help you?"

He isn't a big man, and I tower over him as he draws close. I stretch to my six-foot-two frame, hoping to increase his trepidation.

"Are you the manager?" I know he isn't, and though I've never met the manager, I saw him the night I was here, and I've seen multiple pictures.

He shakes his head. "No, I'm the assistant manager. Agoston isn't in right now."

I wonder how much this guy knows. Does he know he works for a club abducting and trafficking women? Something about his demeanor tells me he doesn't.

"Where is he?"

The man shrugs. "He went on vacation. He's supposed to be back in a couple of days."

"Funny, I thought a manager would need to be in a club to manage it. I guess I should have been a club manager. I'd never have to work." He begins to smile, then sees I'm not joking. Concern etches the corners of his eyes. His mouth opens, but nothing comes out. "It's fine. I don't need him. Nobody should need to go to jail today if you can answer my questions."

His complexion goes white, and his mouth is ajar. I shouldn't take as much pleasure in his discomfort as I do. But it has a purpose—threaten jail time, and people suddenly become more accommodating.

"Wha... what do you want to know?"

"Well, for starters, you had a new bartender working here, Zsuzsa. What happened to her?"

"I... I don't know. She didn't show up for work yesterday."

He's either a great liar, or he knows nothing about it.

"What do you mean she didn't show up for work?"

"Just as I said. She was supposed to work last night, but she never showed."

Bingo. Something *did* happen to her.

"When was the last time anyone saw her?"

He shrugs. "She was here on Saturday night. She walked home after her shift at around three a.m. She was scheduled to come in at six p.m. yesterday but never showed up."

Hmm. She's been missing for less than twenty-four hours. How did Peter know she was taken so fast? *Is he living with her? Or maybe he was supposed to meet her Sunday? But why Ukraine?*

"I'm going to need to look around Agoston's office. Where is it?"

The man shakes his head. "I'm sorry, sir. I can't let you in there. Not without his permission."

I nod, looking around. "Okay, well... As I walked in, I noticed you had some lights hanging down in a hallway. I think I also saw a rat run across the floor in your kitchen. I need to get my buddies with the health department and construction permits over here. You have a lot of problems. Doesn't look like you'll be able to open today. Probably not for a while. These things can take a long time to clear up."

The little man begins to tap his foot on the ground as his face becomes red. He turns around to look up the stairs in the direction he came, then turns back to me. "Okay, I guess you can look around the office."

I give him a wink. "Good choice."

He leads me up the stairs to an office overlooking the dance floor. I follow him into the room.

"Listen, I'm going to need to look around by myself for a few minutes."

He looks at me, shifting his weight from leg to leg, his hand taping his thigh.

"I'm not going to take anything, I promise. I'm just going to look around, and I'd prefer to do it in silence. Your lip smacking is going to drive me crazy."

He starts to object, then thinks better of it, clamping his mouth shut. I can see his mind working. He's probably remembering my previous threat. He shrugs his shoulders and reluctantly leaves the room. The office is spotless. Not a paper in sight. Nothing on the desk. Given that one of their employees has been taken into custody, this isn't all that surprising. If they're smart, any incriminating evidence will be long gone. I wonder if there is any, would I even be able to recognize it?

I sit down at the desk and begin opening the drawers. Nothing but small office supplies and headache medication. I stand and walk to the filing cabinets against the wall. I open the top drawer finding it full of hanging folders. Each is marked with a month and year. I pull out the most recent, December 2000. I head back to the desk, opening the folder in front of me. Nothing exhilarating here: timecards, packing slips for alcohol and food orders, receipts for purchases. I stand and put the folder back. I continue working through the rest, opening the drawers, and reviewing the contents. Each is like the first, nothing incriminating.

I sit back down at the desk. Looking around the office, I realize there isn't anything else. Nothing left to search. *There has to be something. What am I missing?* I think back to the investigation of Andras. He would meet the girls in his restaurant, abduct them, then ship them to Croatia. *Ship them to Croatia. Out of Hungary.* A light dawns, and I jump up to go back to the filing cabinets. I pull out the first folder and put it back on the desk. Flipping through the pages, I find what I'm looking for. Andras had shipped the girls via truck to Croatia. He hid them in food trucks. I find the most recent shipping receipt. It has exactly what I was hoping for, a street address in Kyiv, Ukraine.

Chapter 32

Zsuzsa

"Come to New York with me."

My eyes dart up from the beer glass I'm washing. I search his face, looking for a smile or laugh. Something to indicate he's teasing. He grins, but not in a teasing way. It's more certain. As if he knows this is what I always wanted.

I grew up seeing pictures of the Brooklyn Bridge, the Statue of Liberty, and the Empire State Building. They were beautiful and fascinating. Growing up here, we were taught to fear the West. America and its allies were the enemies, at least according to our government. Their propaganda backfired on me. It made me more curious and interested. I've dreamed of New York City and America.

"Are you serious?" I ask him.

"Of course."

He's looking at me with those light-green eyes. The eyes made me catch my breath the first time they looked at me. He's older than me. Some women might not like it, but I do. I've always been drawn to older men. Something about the confident way they carry themselves. They make me feel safe and comfortable.

"I need to see some friends, and I want you to go with me."

He's looking at me, and I'm so excited that I can't meet his gaze. To go to New York City is beyond my wildest dreams. For him to go and want to take me has me burning up inside. I scrub harder on the beer glass. I don't want him to see how excited I am. The glass slips, and water splashes on my face.

My face is wet. Beads of water are running down my cheek. I take a deep breath as another splash of water hits me. Water is in my nose and mouth. I'm choking, and I begin to cough. I try to move, to wipe the water from my face, but I can't. My arms are bound. I'm in pain. My wrists and ankles are tied tight. Pain emanates from my shoulders and head. My thoughts are cloudy as I fight to open my eyes. A bright light shines overhead. It's too bright, and I shut my eyes. I want to go back to sleep. I don't want to be here. Again, I'm splashed with water. Water runs down my face into my mouth as I try to breathe.

"Zsuzsa."

My eyes flutter open. I recognize the voice. It comes from above. He's standing over me, blocking the light. I try again to open my eyes, and this time I see a familiar face. He leans down so close I can feel his breath. His eyes peer into mine. He raises a hand, and I flinch, afraid he will hit me. But instead, he snaps his fingers. I blink.

"Zsuzsa," he says again.

The fog is lifting. I begin to remember. I try to stand, but I can't. My legs won't move. Something is gripping them. I look down and see ropes tying me to a wooden chair. My arms are behind me. Tied also. He smirks, turning away. He crosses the room, grabbing a wooden chair. Just like the one I'm bound to. He brings it close. It looks like an ordinary kitchen chair with a wicker back. Something you would find in any Hungarian house. He sits down, straddling it, keeping the back toward me. He leans his chin on the top, looking me in the eye.

"Zsuzsa," he says, "can you hear me?"

I realize my eyes are shut again. I force them open. Again, he brings his hand up, ready to snap in my face, but he stops when he sees my eyes are open.

"Zsuzsa, I want to talk to you."

He's staring at me, waiting for me to answer.

"Don't make this hard on yourself. Answer my questions honestly, and this will all go away. Okay?"

I still say nothing. *Where am I? What will go away?*

"I need to hear it. Okay? I don't want to hurt you, Zsuzsa. I really don't. But I will if I have to. Work with me. We need to be honest with each other."

I finally speak: "I don't understand. Where am I? Why am I tied up?"

"I can explain that, but first, I need to ask you some questions."

He nods, studying my face. I nod back.

"Good," he says. He leans back on the chair. "Why did you come back to the club? Who told you to bartend there?"

I frown. "You did. You've been wanting me to come back since I left."

He shakes his head, leaning forward. "No, I asked you to come back and work. But I've been asking you for years. What changed? Who told you to come? Something changed... who told you to accept my offer?"

I shake my head. "Nobody. I needed some extra money."

His hand flashes out so fast I can't even duck. I can only close my eyes as I feel his hand connect with my cheek. I hear a crack and feel my head whip to the side. I see white flashes and feel the heat of his handprint on my face. The chair I'm strapped to wobbles.

His voice has gone cold. "That's a warning, Zsuzsa." He holds up his finger and points it in my face. "I don't like to be lied to." He never raises his voice. Never breaks expression.

I'm conscious of my rapid breathing and heart rate. I take a deep breath, trying to get my bearings.

"I'm going to ask you again, and this time I want honesty. If you lie to me again, things will get much more painful. Who told you to accept my offer to bartend in the club?"

I hesitate, my mind racing. I can't give up Peter. He didn't want me to do it in the first place. He tried to talk me out of it. How can I tell him that Peter came to the restaurant and told me about the missing girls in the club? That it was my idea to go undercover? That I had pestered Peter until he relented? He's growing impatient with my silence. His hand comes up, but this time it's doubled into a fist.

"The police," I nearly shout.

His hand freezes, then comes down to his side. Again, he rests his chin on the top of the chair. "Okay... good. Who with the police?"

Now what? I can't tell him about Peter. I won't betray him. *What's the name of the other guy? Peter's boss?*

"Detective Kovacs."

His eyes narrow. "How did Kovacs find you? Why you?"

"He'd been watching your club for a while. He's been following you. He saw you come to Szépilona a few weeks ago. The last time you came to the restaurant. You ate at the bar. You asked me to come to work at the club on weekends. I don't know how, but he knew about that. He showed up at the restaurant one day. He asked me to call you and accept the offer."

He looks up. His eyes are no longer on me. "But you've never done anything like that before. What did he promise you? Why would you agree?"

This is unexpected, and I'm scrambling. *What does a cop offer a witness? It's not like he could offer me money or a get-out-of-jail-free card. Jail! That's it.*

"He said he could make my criminal record go away."

"What criminal record?"

Exactly. What criminal record?

"A couple of years ago, I got some DUIs. My license was revoked. That's why I don't have a car anymore." *Actually, I've never had a car. I hope he doesn't know that.*

He nods. He's buying it. "So, he says he can get rid of those for you. Take them off your record if you work at the club. And what did he want you to do at the club?"

"Nothing. Just work there and answer his questions."

"What questions? What would he ask you?"

I shrug. "I didn't work there long. He'd call me the next day, asking who I worked with and who I saw. If I saw anything unusual. Stuff like that."

He raises an eyebrow. "And did you see anything unusual?"

I shake my head. "No, nothing."

He's been so calm that I've allowed myself to relax. That's why I don't see it coming when he whips his hand toward me, slapping me hard across the face. My cheek is numb, but this new assault lights it on fire again. This time he hits me so hard my head flips to the side, and I feel the chair wobble then lean to the side. I cry out in pain as I hit the floor. Forgetting my hands are tied, I try to correct myself. The movement sends jolts of pain through my shoulders. The rope is burning my flesh. I close my eyes, flinching as he stands over me, expecting another blow. But it doesn't come. Instead, he grabs my chair and sits me back up. I open my eyes, and tears spill out, running out of the corners of my eyes.

His mouth turns up on one side as he shakes his head. "Didn't I tell you not to lie to me? This would be much easier if you stayed honest with me."

I have no idea what he thinks I'm lying about. Was it about not seeing anything? I really hadn't seen anything. But he thinks I have. What does he think I know? Women have been going missing in the club. He knows I know that. That's why I was asked to go undercover. It must be something else. I think back to my last night in the club. Bela walked me out. Was that it? Something I said to him?

He stands, comes over to me, and pulls my chair back up with me attached. The movement erupts a new cascade of pain. "Let's try this again, Zsuzsa. What did you tell Kovacs about the club?"

"Nothing," I cry. His hand comes up again to strike, and I blurt out, "Bela was stealing from the club."

Surprise registers on his face, and his hand freezes. He's sitting there with a confused look, his hand in the air.

"What did you say?"

"Bela... he's stealing alcohol from the club. I told the police."

A smile plays at the corner of his lips, eventually spreading. He throws back his head and laughs. He's laughing so hard that I wonder if he's lost his mind. Finally, he gets his laughter under control and looks at me, shaking his head. The look is odd. It's not anger or happiness. It's fake empathy.

"Oh, Zsuzsa, you are unlucky."

The door behind him opens, and another guy comes in. He approaches, leans down, and whispers in Agoston's ear.

Agoston glares at him, pulling away. "What are you whispering for? Who cares if she hears."

"He's on the phone."

"Yeah? Right now?"

The guy nods, and Agoston stands and leaves the room. The other guy follows him out, shutting the door behind him. I'm alone now. I look around, surveying my surroundings. It's dark. A single light hangs above my head. The walls are too far away for me to make out anything in the shadows. The floor is dusty concrete. A dirty, balled-up rag sits beside me, a dark stain tracing the outside. *Where am I?* They've left me alone with no fear of me escaping. There's nothing for me to use to cut my binds. Nowhere to go. But that's not what worries me the most. My mouth is unbound. No gag. *They don't care if I scream. There's nobody around to hear me.*

Agoston will return soon. *What's he going to do next? Why am I still alive?* They just need information from me. What did Agoston mean, "Who cares if she hears?" *Why would he not care? Why doesn't it matter if I learn new things?* I draw a breath as realization comes. He doesn't care because I won't be alive much longer. They're going to kill me.

The door reopens, and I flinch. Agoston walks back in. "Well, Zsuzsa, it seems we'll have company soon. Your friends are on their way. Too bad they won't find you."

What does that mean? He's going to kill me. I need something to make him want to keep me alive. He's walking toward me.

"Agoston... you know me," I plead. "There's more I can tell you."

He smirks, and it's the most frightening thing I've ever seen. I've said the wrong thing.

Chapter 33

Peter

Peter stands outside a large apartment building in Kyiv. After finding Renata and talking with Larysa and her grandmother, he convinced all the women to help him find where Renata had been found. He needed all of them; Larysa to translate for the grandmother, Agnes to support and comfort Renata, and the grandmother and Renata for obvious reasons. After the kind old woman led them to the neighborhood, Renata retraced her steps to the apartment building she had been held captive in. She was terrified, her anxiety growing with each step. When she identified the building, she looked away and couldn't didn't gaze at it again. Seeing what it was doing to her, Peter didn't press her and took the girls to a hotel. After getting them settled, he came back to the building. He knows there's no time to lose. Multiple women are being held in there, possibly including Zsuzsa.

Peter enters the building and heads for the fourth floor. Renata wasn't sure, but she thought she had been detained there. Rather than take the elevator, he takes the stairs, hoping to get familiar with the lay of the building. As he reaches the fourth floor, he stops to listen. It would be nice to have backup, but he can't contact the local police, and Kovacs is too far away.

In Hungary, the traffickers are working with someone on the force. He would be a fool to assume the same isn't true in Ukraine. The building has a hallway running down the middle of each floor with three apartment doors along each wall. Renata said her abductors were watching TV in the front room, and she could hear it from the hallway. He walks down the hall, moving close to each door, listening. Two of the six doors have audible sounds from within. The voices are repetitive, indicating either TV or radio. Without seeing them, he has no way of knowing which.

He considers knocking on each door, but then what? He doesn't speak Ukrainian. A man going door to door speaking English or Hungarian would bring too much attention. His only choice is to wait and see if one of the men comes out. He moves back to the staircase, going up a flight of stairs to the fifth floor. Over the next hour, several people pass him on the stairs. Both look at him curiously but thankfully say nothing. He worries someone will try to talk to him and realize he's a foreigner. Finally, he hears the bing of the elevator. It stops on the fourth floor. He descends the stairs keeping out of sight. From where he stands now, the entire hallway is visible. A young man in his early twenties walks down the hall. He's tall, at least six feet, and thin. He's wearing a dark coat and a knit cap. He stops midway down the hall, slips a key into the door, and walks in.

Peter descends the rest of the stairs and moves down the hallway toward the door. As he draws near, he can hear movement within.

Like someone is rearranging furniture. Peter puts his ear to the door. Realizing his back is now to the stairway and the elevator, he switches positions. His right ear is now on the door listening. The last thing he wants is someone coming up from behind. Listening closely, the significant movement has stopped, and he hears a whooshing sound, like the guy is sweeping or mopping. For the first time, Peter smells the distinct odor of bleach. Renata said the apartment was a mess. Why would the guy be cleaning? Maybe this wasn't the right place. Maybe Renata had been wrong. It wasn't on the fourth floor.

The sound of sweeping stops, and the footsteps grow louder. He's approaching the door. Peter speed walks back to the staircase. When the door opens, he changes his tempo. He strolls down the hallway like he's out for a Sunday afternoon walk. He continues to the stairs and begins to climb to the next level. Reaching the middle landing, he turns and looks back. The man has a couple of boxes in his arms. He heads toward the elevator, and Peter continues up to the fifth floor. A chime sounds below, indicating the elevator has arrived. Peter turns around and heads back down the stairs, through the hallway, to the apartment door. He knows what he's about to do is dangerous, but he doesn't care. Peter takes out his Swiss Army knife and picks the lock, a skill he learned during his time in New York City. After busting a prolific thief, he convinced him to teach him in exchange for dropping one of the charges. Peter had found the skill valuable, making use of it several times. The lock pops, and he knows he's in, pushing open the door.

The floor plan of the apartment matches Renata's description. A kitchen and living room lie opposite each other. A hallway runs from the front door to the back of the apartment with two doors, one on either side. Everything matches her description, except this apartment is spotless. No pizza boxes or beer cans. It's bare too. No TV or radio. It looks like someone has recently moved out. He heads down the hallway to one of the bedrooms. Reaching the door, he pushes it open and looks in. The room is crammed with four beds. There's barely space for anyone to walk. One of the bed frames is broken, with the frame lying on the ground. This is it. This is the apartment she was kept in. But the beds are empty. *Where did the other girls go?*

Peter steps back into the hallway, but as he does, he hears footsteps outside. Someone is coming through the door. He steps back into the room, silently closing the door behind him. He can hear the thud of footsteps entering the apartment. Peter listens carefully, barely breathing. The footsteps move around the apartment. He reaches inside his coat, taking out his gun. The last thing he wants is to get in a firefight with this guy in the middle of an apartment, especially in a foreign country. Killing the guy wouldn't get him closer to finding the girls or Zsuzsa.

The footsteps remain in the front of the apartment. Peter hears the guy moving things around. *He must be looking for something.* Abruptly, the footsteps stop. *Maybe he's found it.* The footsteps start again, moving away from the kitchen toward the living room. Again, Peter hears the sound of something heavy sliding around. *Is he searching for something?* *Or did he bring something in?* The footsteps start again, but now they're getting louder and closer. He's coming down the hall. Peter steps to the side of the door, pressing his back to the wall. He fingers his gun, releasing the safety. He tries to control his breathing, but it sounds as loud as a locomotive.

The footsteps stop outside the bedroom door. *What's he waiting for? Maybe he knows I'm inside?* Perhaps he's preparing to come through the door. Peter holds his breath, fighting for silence. Finally, the doorknob turns, and the door swings open. On the opposite wall sits a mirror. The mirror is angled so Peter can see the doorframe and the man standing in it. The man isn't looking in the room, though. He's looking down, reaching inside his jacket. Something is buzzing. He's getting a call on his mobile phone. He pushes a button and raises it to his ear, speaking Ukrainian.

The room is silent, and Peter can hear the voice on the other end of the line. He can't hear what is said, not that it would matter. It's in Ukrainian. Whatever it is, it's clear the person isn't happy. He's yelling at the man. The man turns and walks away from the bedroom. He goes down the hallway and stops in front of the exterior door to the apartment, repeating, "*Tak. Tak.*"

Peter hears the shuffle of a box and the front door opening. The guy is leaving. As the door shuts, Peter exits the bedroom and walks to the end of the hallway. He stops at the front door calculating how long he will need to wait before the guy clears the hallway and won't be able to see him leaving. He counts to fifteen Mississippi, turns the knob, and opens the door just a crack leaning out and looking toward the elevator. Nobody's there.

Peter runs to the stairs, stepping lightly. He's treading a line between losing the guy and being seen. He hustles down the stairs, slowing to a walking pace as he reaches the second floor. The guy should be easy to identify; he's carrying boxes, and Peter saw him in the mirror. As Peter nears the bottom floor, he sees the elevator door is shut. He clears the final set of stairs and exits the building. It's now late afternoon in Kyiv, and shadows are stretching east away from the sun. It must have snowed a few days ago because crusty, white snow covers the ground. The walks are clear but wet. Melted snow and ice are remnants of a bright, sunny day. The melted water is reforming ice pockets now that the sun is setting. Peter will have to watch his step to keep from losing his balance. Across the street, he identifies his man. He's walking toward a white Volkswagen van carrying boxes. Peter looks around. Luckily, this is a busy part of the city, and a taxi is parked a block away. He runs toward the cab, occasionally looking over his shoulder to keep tabs on the man. As he reaches the taxi, he motions for the driver to roll down his window. The driver looks at him with surprise.

"Do you speak English?" he asks the driver.

The man stares blankly.

"English," Peter repeats louder and more emphatically.

The driver shrugs. Peter takes that to mean *a little*. He looks over his shoulder. The abductor starts his van and flips on his lights. Peter opens the back door to the taxi and slides in.

"Follow the white van," he tells the driver, leaning over the seat and pointing to it.

The driver turns around to stare at Peter.

"Volkswagen," Peter tells him, emphasizing every syllable.

The van is coming right toward them. Peter points again, saying, "White Volkswagen, follow. White Volkswagen, follow."

The driver looks in the direction Peter is pointing and sees the van; understanding dawns on him. He gives Peter a thumbs-up, throws the car into gear, and pulls out to follow. Peter sits back and sucks in a huge gulp of air.

Ten minutes later, Peter sits up in the back seat of the taxi, watching the van turn into a deserted industrial park. A solitary building sits in the lot. It looks old and vacant. Peter motions for the driver to continue. After they pass the building and are out of eyesight, he instructs him to park along the road behind a set of pine trees. The drive hadn't been easy, but they made it work. Their lack of a common language forced them to communicate in a jumble of English, Russian, and body language.

Now Peter motions to his watch, holding up ten fingers. The driver nods, pointing to the watch and holding up ten fingers. Peter exits the car and walks under the trees toward the building. After crossing under the canopy of branches, he reaches an old fence and crouches down, keeping his eyes on the building. The guy from the minivan has parked. He climbs out and walks to the back of the van opening the trunk. The door to the industrial building opens, and two guys come out. Both are young, in their early twenties. Both look to be athletic. They join the driver at the van picking up boxes. Both are wearing jackets, but as they move to pick up the boxes, their jackets ride up, exposing their waists. Both have guns.

Another man comes out but makes no move to help. Instead, he's yelling at the driver. Chastising him for something. Probably the same guy who had called on the phone. The men carry the boxes inside, passing the boss. The boss turns to follow them, stopping to give Peter a perfect view. Peter feels his pulse increase as he looks at him. *I know him. But how?* The man enters the building shutting the door. Peter remains crouched in the field, running through possibilities. *Was he on the train? Was he at the hotel where Agnes and Renata are staying?* Neither of those seems right. Peter turns and heads back to the taxi, hoping the driver understood to stay. Before he reaches it, he realizes where he's seen the man. He was in Szépilona. He was sitting at Zsuzsa's bar the second time he had gone there. *How had he gotten here? Who is he?* The realization comes with a surge of relief. If he's here, Zsuzsa likely is also.

After arriving back at the hotel, Peter hears the phone ring and the sound of Detective Kovacs's unmistakable voice.

"Peter? Where the hell are you?"

Peter's expecting this. He left Budapest a couple of days ago without telling Kovacs.

"I'm in Kyiv."

"Are you looking for Zsuzsa?"

Peter flinches at the mention of her name. "What do you know?"

Kovacs hesitates. "Isn't that why you went to Ukraine?"

"No."

"Why did you go then?"

"Zsuzsa was supposed to meet me on Sunday morning at a café, but she never came. I went by her house, but she wasn't home. Do you know where she is? What do you know?"

Kovacs hesitates again. "Uh... well, nobody seems to know where she is. She worked Saturday night in the club, then hasn't been seen since. The director got a call that you'd crossed the Ukrainian border, and I thought you'd gone to get her. I found a packing slip in the office of the club with a Kyiv address on it."

Peter's mind is racing. "Lajos, I need you up here right now. I need you in Kyiv."

Kovacs seems testy. "Peter, what are you doing there? Why did you go?"

"I got a call from Agnes. She told me Renata had called her. I went over and talked with Renata and found out she was in Kyiv. I figured if they took her here, they likely brought Zsuzsa also. I got on a train, and Agnes and I found Renata. She showed me where she'd been held, and I followed one of the abductors to an industrial park outside the city."

"What's the address of the industrial park?" Kovacs asks.

Peter looks down at his notes, repeating the address, butchering the pronunciation.

Kovacs snaps his fingers. "That's exactly the address I found on the packing slip. I'll leave right away. Don't do anything without me. Do you hear me, Peter? Nothing!"

"They have Zsuzsa. I have to save her."

"You can't save her if you're dead and they disappear again. Promise me you won't do anything. You'll wait for me."

Peter nods. Kovacs is right. There are too many of them for him to take out alone.

"Promise me?"

"I promise. But Lajos?"

"Yes?"

"Don't tell anyone you're coming. Nobody on the team. Not even the director."

"Peter, you know I have to tell him."

"You can't tell him. You can't tell anyone. We don't know who we can trust. Someone could let them know we're coming."

Kovacs lets out a long sigh. "Toth will know I'm heading to Ukraine. Even if I don't tell him. The border patrol alerts him anytime one of his people crosses the border."

"Then you have to come up with a different ID. Something that can get you across without them knowing who you are. We can't afford for them to know."

Kovacs is again silent. "Okay, I'll figure something out. I'll be there soon. Wait for me."

The line goes dead. Peter hangs up, walks to the bed's edge, and sits down. Near the industrial park, he could feel Zsuzsa was there. He could sense her presence somehow. The guy he recognized had her. He was sure of it. Waiting for Kovacs was going to be the longest day of his life. He just hoped it wouldn't be too late when they raided the building.

Chapter 34
Director Toth

"Father, who's Tony Curtis?"

I'm so lost in thought I don't realize my daughter is talking to me. I only vaguely hear her. I continue to stare at my plate in front of me. She taps me on the shoulder, and I turn to look up from my meal. She's no longer looking at me. She's looking at her mother, and the look on her face says, "He's doing it again."

"What?" I ask her.

She turns back to me. "I said, who's Tony Curtis?"

"He's an actor. Why?"

"Like an actor in America?"

"Yes."

What an odd question. But then again, my daughter, Ildiko, always asks me strange questions. When Ildiko is around, I feel like I'm Alex Trebek, the host of *Jeopardy!*, constantly hearing her say "who is" or "what is" to me. I guess I should be flattered, not annoyed. She thinks I have all the answers. I think she imagines me to be an encyclopedia. "Why are you asking about him?"

Her brow furrows, and she looks confused. "That doesn't make any sense." She's no longer talking to me.

"What doesn't make sense, honey?"

My wife has jumped into the conversation, seeing my frustration is building.

Ildiko turns back to her mother. "Well, I'm supposed to do a report in school on a famous Hungarian. And the teacher assigned me Tony Curtis."

Now I understand. "Well, technically, Tony Curtis is Hungarian. At least his family is. His real name is Bernát Schwartz. He was born in New York. But he never lived here. I don't know why your teacher would even include him."

Just another example of the problems in the country. Why wouldn't the teacher require students to learn about native Hungarians? People who actually lived in Hungary, not just those with Hungarian lineage. Even people like Zsa Zsa Gabor and József Pulitzer were at least born in Hungary. They actually lived in Hungary for several years. Zsa Zsa was Miss Hungary. That's how she was discovered. Since the wall came down in Berlin, Western influence has been overwhelming Budapest. I don't like it.

Ildiko barely reacts to that. She's used to me talking about the problems with the West.

I stand from the table. "I've got to go make a call."

My wife, Eszter, starts clearing the dishes. I walk down the hallway and enter the study. I close the door, sit at the desk, and dial the number. Almost immediately, the phone is answered, and I hear a familiar voice.

"Hi, It's me. Look, something's going on. Peter had already crossed the border, and when I asked Kovacs about it, he acted as if he might already know. Those two might be working together. I need you to try and find out what they know. What they're involved in. I'm beginning to think I can't trust them."

The voice on the other end is calm and collected. It's precisely why they're suitable for this. "No problem, boss. I'll find out."

Chapter 35

Peter

Peter sits waiting in the lobby of the hotel. He can't help it. He finds himself continually checking his watch. Summoning some Jedi mind trick he doesn't possess to make it move faster. It's only been twelve hours since he talked with Kovacs, but it feels like weeks. Even though he hasn't slept more than a few minutes here and there in two days, he tossed and turned in his hotel bed. Zsuzsa occupied his thoughts. This morning, he gave up and got out of bed. After checking on Renata and Agnes, he came downstairs and ordered some tea. He wants to know the instant Kovacs arrives.

He looks at his watch again, and although he's done it endlessly for the last several hours, this time, it distracts him. He loves this watch, not only because it reminds him of flying but because of how he got it. His wife, Karen, gave it to him. Something about the watch and the hotel lobby puts him back twenty years. They were married in Manhattan at Trinity Church. The bride's wedding party exceeded the groom's by five to one. Karen was one of four children from a large extended family. She was also beloved by everyone who knew her. She was a nurse at Manhattan General, and every doctor and nurse came. Nobody wanted to miss her wedding. Peter, on the other hand, had no family present. He has two siblings, both older. His brother was killed when they were young, and he hadn't seen his sister in years. The only people in his wedding party were buddies from the NYPD.

It was September in New York City, and the leaves had turned orange, yellow, and brown. It was 1979. New York City was dirty, and crime levels were at an all-time high. Ten million people practically living on top of each other. Peter could remember watching Karen as the photographer snapped pictures of her outside the church. She looked like an angel in her white dress. A beacon of light set against the backdrop of substantial gray buildings and filthy streets. He remembered watching her, never wanting the day to end. He marveled at his luck. How could this woman, this angel, have chosen him?

A few hours later, they sat with legs and arms intertwined on their flight to LA before finishing the leg to Lihue, Hawaii. Peter had first seen a picture of the Hawaiian Islands in school. It was in black and white, but he still found himself mesmerized by it. Several years later, he watched a movie filmed on the Islands. From that time forward, he promised himself if he ever got married, he would honeymoon in Hawaii. After Karen had agreed to marry him, he hired a travel agent and got her working on Hawaiian options. She found a tremendous deal on airfare to Kauai. The flights were long and took all night, but they slept most of the way tangled up together. They arrived in Kauai rested and ready to go. They were surrounded by dewy, moist air and sunshine as they stepped off the plane. They picked up their rental car and looked for something to eat. Deciding to head to the coast, they found a cute restaurant called Duke's next to the harbor. They sat on the deck, watching boats sail in, and surfers play in the waves. After their meal, they headed up the coast to their Princeville hotel. The drive was beautiful, and they nearly stopped multiple times along the way, the draw of the beach and waves pulling them like a magnet.

After arriving at the hotel, they put on their swimming suits and asked the concierge for a beach recommendation. He recommended Hideaway Beach, just a ten-minute walk away. He failed to mention the treacherous climb down to the beach. Looking down from the top, Peter worried it would be too much for Karen. But she pushed his worries aside, climbing down in front of him. The ropes and steps made the descent doable, if not still dangerous. They reached the bottom without incident.

They spread their towels along the sand, sitting down and looking at the vast ocean. To their left sat the Kaanapali coast, the site of Bali Hai from the movie *South Pacific*. Its rugged mountains and lush rainforest were picturesque. To their right sat the cliffs of Princeville and the lava-rock region called Queens Bath. Although this was somewhere he had always dreamed of being, he enjoyed watching Karen more. He loved the wonder he saw in her eyes.

After sitting around in awe for a few minutes, Karen turned to him with a twinkle in her eye. "You know, we're alone on this beach and still haven't consummated our marriage."

They consummated their love on the beach, in the water, and at the hotel later that night. They had to make up for all the flying. The following day, he sat in the hotel lobby, waiting for her to come down drinking his tea. That week in Hawaii had been incomprehensible. How could a simple Hungarian boy ever dream of something like that? Experience something so wonderful. For nearly twenty years, they were together. Not every day was perfect. They had challenges and adversity. But Peter considered himself lucky every day of those twenty years. Every day until the day she never came home. Until they found her lifeless body in the New York City alleyway. Until someone stole her from him.

Her murder is still unsolved, but he can't help but feel responsible. He's sure someone killed her as retribution. Knowing that taking Karen from him would be worse than losing his own life. Living in a world without her would be hell on earth. That was over a year ago, and every day he wakes without her feels like a knife stabbed into his chest.

Then he met Zsuzsa. He wasn't looking for someone. He thought he'd never find a woman who excited him like Karen. Zsuzsa was different. But she carried the same spunk. He liked the way she teased him. The look in her eyes as she watched him. Nobody could ever replace Karen, but Zsuzsa had reduced some of the hurt. Some of the longing he felt for her.

Now Zsuzsa's missing, and just like Karen, he's to blame. Why is it that any woman he becomes close to and cares for gets killed? *No, not again. I'm not going to let this happen again. Zsuzsa won't die because of me.*

He stands from the table and stalks across the lobby. Not this time. He'll find a taxi and go back to the factory. He has to save her.

He isn't going to let her die because of him. A black Mercedes pulls up as he exits the lobby and walks outside into the frosty air. Detective Kovacs Lajos steps out. He looks at Peter, and that's explanation enough. He knows Peter's patience has evaporated. He's arrived just in time.

He slaps Peter on the shoulder and says, "Come on. Let's go get her."

Chapter 36

Peter

Peter sits in the back seat of the Mercedes, a million questions running through his head. After Kovacs pulled up, he directed Peter into the car's back seat and went to talk with someone in the car behind them. Kovacs had ignored Peter's wishes and brought reinforcements with him. Beyond the vehicle Peter sits in, there are three more black Mercedes and a couple of local police cars. After a few minutes, Kovacs returns, opens the door, and slides in beside Peter. Kovacs tells the driver to go, and he pulls out into traffic. The driver is a bald, muscular man who speaks Hungarian and English.

Peter can't wait any longer. "I thought we agreed to keep this quiet?"

Kovacs pulls at his lip. "Yeah... about that. I couldn't see a way around bringing reinforcements. I didn't have a way to reach you, so I made the call. Sorry."

Peter turns away from him. He understands the need for more guns but knows this trafficking group is well-placed. Like Hungary, they likely infiltrated the Ukrainian police force. Their tentacles might reach all the way into the government. Kovacs's decision to include them could be Zsuzsa's undoing. The traffickers could have received a tip and been gone.

Peter turns back, his temper flaring. Kovacs sees it, raising his hand to cut him off.

"You don't have to say it. You're right. It might have been a mistake. But I want you to step back and see the whole picture. I didn't like our odds. The two of us against six guys or more in that warehouse? They know the layout and terrain. Plus, as I told you, Toth is watching the borders. I wasn't sure how I could get across on my own without him being notified."

Peter exhales, feeling his anger subside. He's not happy but understands.

"So, I placed a call to Interpol. I have a contact there. That's who I brought with me. They were able to get me a flight here. No passport required. And because the operation isn't in Hungary, Toth hasn't been informed. Nobody in Hungary knows I've left, for now."

Peter is relieved but still worries about the Ukrainian involvement. There are more than Interpol officers with them.

"What about the police here? The traffickers have probably infiltrated the local force."

Kovacs nods. "Yeah, they probably have. I told Interpol the same thing. They assured me they would involve as few local officers as possible, and those they did would pass a background check."

Peter has his doubts, but what can he do now? They're coming, like it or not.

"Plus," Kovacs says, "since your call last night, Interpol has been watching the warehouse. Nobody has gone in or out without them knowing."

Peter isn't sure how much that would matter if Zsuzsa is already inside and dead, but he doesn't say it. After another five minutes, they pull up down the road from the warehouse. Kovacs tells Peter to come with him, and they get out. A group of Interpol officials and several Ukrainian police stand together in a group. An Interpol officer takes the lead. This group comprises native Hungarian and Ukrainian speakers and perhaps other languages. English is the most universal of the languages. Kovacs speaks only marginal English. Kovacs gives Peter a look several times, and Peter whispers a quick translation.

"We're going to take them by force," the Interpol agent explains. "We've counted six guys in all. We know they're carrying handguns and expect larger firepower inside. We have no intelligence on the number of girls being held. Our best guess is anywhere from three to twelve." He holds up a diagram of the building. All the members of the team crowd around to see better. "We're going to breach the side door here."

Peter notices it's the same door he saw the familiar man from the bar and the other traffickers use.

"Like any situation where hostages might be present," the agent says, "our best hope of success is speed and accuracy. Take them by surprise." He turns to Kovacs and Peter. "We'll go in first, then you two can follow. The girls are likely Hungarian or at least were taken in Hungary. We'll need your language to help calm them. Once the building is secure, we'll call you in."

The agent returns to his men, giving them final instructions before heading toward the warehouse. Peter feels a pump of adrenaline radiate through his body. It's all he can do not to run straight for the building. Zsuzsa might be inside. He could be seeing her in mere minutes. The question was whether she'd still be alive.

The Interpol agent commands Peter and Kovacs to stay at the top of the driveway as the remaining team circles the building. Peter counts seven Interpol agents and eight Ukrainian police. Each is geared in heavy armor. Once everyone is in position, the head agent gives the signal, and they breach the exterior door. Agents roll canisters of tear gas into the open door. Screams emanate from the building, followed by several volleys of gunfire. Agents pour inside from every angle. Finally, after what seems like an eternity, the head agent emerges, waving an all-clear to Peter and Kovacs. Peter takes off running. Reaching the exterior door, he ducks inside. His nostrils are assaulted by an array of smells. The tear gas is dissipating but is still prominent. The Interpol agents are still clearing the warehouse, room to room, but Kovacs and Peter are pointed down a hallway where some of the girls have been found.

The first room holds a group of five, all still sleeping. Each has an IV extending from their arm. Peter has to wonder how heavily sedated someone must be to sleep through tear gas and gunfire. He examines each woman. Zsuzsa isn't among them.

"Peter, keep moving. I'll look after them. Find her."

Peter exits the room, moving farther down the hallway. He steps over two male bodies on the floor. Both are either badly wounded or dead. He recognizes them. One is the driver he followed yesterday. The other helped carry boxes from the van to the building. Reaching the end of the hallway, he finds a large, dark room. The only light is natural, leaking through the windows at the top near the roof. Through the shadows, he can see several Interpol agents have four traffickers handcuffed and kneeling before them. That's six men, counting the two dead in the hallway. He looks face-to-face but doesn't see the man who sat at Zsuzsa's bar in Szépilona.

To his right, Peter hears someone call out in English, "We've got a woman in here."

Peter's hopes soar. The agent said *woman*. Zsuzsa is a woman, and these young ladies would be considered girls in comparison. He runs to the sound of the voice. The agent moves out, letting Peter in. As he enters the small room, he exhales his held breath. Even through the dark, he recognizes the blond hair and soft curves. It's Zsuzsa. She's tied to a chair. Bound at the ankles. Her arms are bound behind her back. Peter rushes to her, his anxiety growing. Her head is down, limp. *Is she dead? He* kneels in front of her, putting his hand on her cheek. Her skin is cold. He slides his hand under her chin, raising her face to look at him. The movement causes her eyes to flutter, then close. Tears come to his eyes. She's alive! He reaches inside his pocket, feeling for his knife. She isn't doing well, and he needs to get her out of here. He cuts the ropes holding her ankles first, then her hands behind her. She slumps to the side, and he hugs her to him, helping her to the ground. Without thinking, he tosses his knife to the side. Gently gripping her, he rolls her over, face up.

Her eyes flutter again, but this time they stay open. Peter can see them focus. Recognition plays on her face as she looks at him.

"I'm here," he whispers.

A smile spreads across her cracked lips. She takes a breath and opens her mouth, trying to speak. Nothing comes out. She's so weak.

Peter feels something hard and cold jab into his temple. He hears the cock of a gun in his ear.

"Stand up slowly," commands a voice.

The voice speaks to him in Hungarian, not English.

As Peter stands, his loathing for the man rises like dirty bathwater. This man has tortured Zsuzsa and now has him.

The man steps back from Peter, holding the gun extended toward him.

"Well, this is fortunate," the man says. "I thought I'd have to use Zsuzsa as my leverage out of here. But I think you might be an even better option."

Without warning, he swings his gun away from Peter, aiming instead toward Zsuzsa. Peter feels his heart sink as the sound of a gunshot reverberates. But something's wrong. The sound originated from farther away. The man screams, his gun flying across the room. He looks at his hand and sees a stream of blood pouring from it. He drops to his knees, crying out in agony, gripping his hand. Kovacs rushes in, his gun trained on the man.

"Stay on your knees!" he commands.

Kovacs comes to stand over him, his gun trained on his head. "Get Zsuzsa out of here."

Chapter 37

Peter

Peter sits in the back of the ambulance, holding Zsuzsa's hand. She's badly dehydrated. The EMTs hooked her to an IV to get fluids back into her body. After evaluating her, the emergency response team said it had been at least two days since she had been given anything to eat or drink. Holding her hand, he examines her wrists. Her skin is raw from the constant pressure of the ropes. Looking at her ankles, he finds rope burns. She's been through so much. Peter feels his eyes become cloudy. Although bruised, she's alive. He says a silent prayer of thanks to God.

The ambulance hits a bump, and Zsuzsa's eyes flutter. She turns her head, looking at him. Their eyes lock. She takes a breath, opening her mouth, and tries to speak. This time only a tiny whisper escapes. Peter stands and leans closer, his face inches from hers.

She inhales and tries again. "What took you so long?"

A smile plays at the corners of her mouth, and her eyes dance as she watches him. She's teasing, but her words hit him like a thousand-pound truck. Had he taken any longer, he would have lost her for good.

She wants humor, but all he feels is guilt. "I'm so sorry, Zsuzsa. I'm so sorry."

Her eyebrows crease as she says, "Why? You didn't do it."

How simplistic. Granted, he didn't abduct her or tie her up. He didn't torture her or deprive her of food and water. But doesn't a commanding officer in the military bear some responsibility for the death of the soldiers under him? He had allowed her to be put in the position. He had agreed to have her work in a place where he knew she was in danger.

"Agoston knew things," Zsuzsa says, deflecting the focus.

"What?"

"Agoston, the club manager. The guy who held me. He knew things."

"What things?"

"Things. Only someone in the police..." It was a labor for her to speak. "Someone in the police... told him. He knew things."

Peter nods. This confirms his suspicions.

"Are you in pain?" the paramedic asks in English. Zsuzsa looks at Peter.

"Are you in pain?" Peter translates.

Zsuzsa nods, and the paramedic stands. She unhooks the fluid bag from the IV, then connects a small tube to the IV injecting it into her arm. She turns back to Peter. "That will help her sleep. She's probably exhausted."

Peter thanks her, but as he focuses back on Zsuzsa, he finds she's already back asleep.

After arriving at the hospital, the doctors take Zsuzsa for evaluation. Peter realizes he hasn't eaten in hours. He leaves the waiting room and wanders around the hospital, unable to read any of the signs and unsure who he can ask. Eventually, he finds his way to the cafeteria. When he walks in, he's surprised to find Kovacs.

"How's our girl doing?" Kovacs asks after Peter picks up some food and sits across from him at the table.

"She's being evaluated by the doctors. We'll see. But she's exhausted and hurting."

Kovacs bites his lip as he looks down at his sandwich. "I'm thrilled about how this turned out. I don't know if I would have been able to forgive myself otherwise."

Peter knows what he means. He's experiencing those same feelings. Peter had told Kovacs of Zsuzsa's connection to the club. It had been Kovacs who had pushed Peter to take her up on her offer to scope it out.

"Hey, I didn't get a chance to thank you yet."

Kovacs waves him away. "Eh, that was nothing. Lucky shot. I'm just glad I was there."

Peter shakes his head. "No, it was more than something. You saved either my life or Zsuzsa's and possibly both. You also did it in a way that we can take him into custody. That's no small thing."

Kovacs nods. "Yeah, taking him alive was pretty good. Now we've actually got someone who's connected. I'm anxious to see what we can learn from him. See what he knows."

"Has he said anything yet?"

Kovacs shakes his head. "Not yet. But he will. We'll get him back to Hungary and make him talk."

"He knows who our rat is in the police force."

Kovacs looks at Peter, his eyes piercing. "Are you sure?"

Peter tells him about his conversation with Zsuzsa in the ambulance.

Kovacs sets down his fork and folds his arms, leaning back. "We're going to have to be really careful with him. Keep it quiet until we get him to talk. Tomorrow I'll be taking him to Hungary. I'll take Renata and Agnes with me. Why don't you stay here with Zsuzsa? Get a flight back to Budapest once she's ready."

Chapter 38

Peter

"Peter, come with me."

Peter sits at his desk, head in his hands, in the bullpen of the Human Trafficking Task Force of the Hungarian National Police Station. Last night he had arrived back in Budapest. After talking with Kovacs in the hospital, Peter returned to Zsuzsa's room. He didn't want her to be alone. Other than her hospital bed and a chair in the corner, the room was bare. She slept for twelve hours straight, and Peter, sitting on a chair, did his best to get some rest. When she woke, she begged him to take her home. He agreed, wanting out of there himself. The doctors had other ideas. They wanted to keep her longer for observation. Zsuzsa was having none of it. Peter finally convinced them to let him take her home. He brought her to the airport that night, getting them on a flight back to Budapest.

He had always loved flying, having dreamed of being a pilot in his younger days. Now, he embraced the novelty of boarding a plane in one city and exiting in a different one, sometimes not even in the same country. But this flight was so much more. From the time they sat down, Zsuzsa never stopped touching him. Beyond thanking him endlessly for rescuing her, he saw the appreciation in her eyes. She kept her arm through his, leaned her leg across to his side, and rested her head on his shoulder. The chemistry was like it had been on their first date. They gazed into each other's eyes as they talked, barely aware there were other passengers. Not caring that there were. When they landed in Budapest, Peter contemplated offering the pilot money to circle the city. He didn't want to let her go. To lose the connection he felt.

They walked out of Ferihegy Airport and called a taxi. Living in different parts of the city, they had reached a separation point. It didn't make sense for them to share a taxi. As he called the cab and opened the door for her, he looked into her eyes. She was exhausted. She had been through so much and needed rest. He told her to take the taxi, and he would call another one. Before she slid into the back seat, Peter reached under her chin, raising her face to his. As he stared into those beautiful eyes, he leaned down and kissed her.

Now, sitting at his desk, her lips are all he can think about.

"Peter? Anyone home?" Kovacs says.

"Sorry. A lot on my mind."

"Yeah, I can tell. I have to go report to the director. He wants you to come along."

"Okay."

Peter finds that odd but stands, pushing away from his desk. He falls into step beside Kovacs as they walk down the hall toward the director's office.

"He wants a report on Kyiv. I'm not sure how much he knows."

Peter's surprised Kovacs hasn't spoken with him yet. He arrived home a day before Peter.

Peter has never been to the director's office and isn't sure where they're going. Kovacs stops in front of an office door and knocks. On the wall beside the door, Peter notices a black plaque with gold lettering identifying the office's occupant.

"Come," calls a stern voice from within.

Kovacs opens the door, and Peter follows him inside. Director Toth sits behind a large cherrywood desk. The desk holds a stack of folders, a telephone, a computer monitor, and a lamp. The director has a pair of glasses perched on the end of his nose.

"Have a seat. I'll be right with you," the director says without looking up.

He has a folder on his desk and sits hunched over it, engrossed. Peter and Kovacs take the chairs opposite the desk. As Peter sits, he feels the plush softness of the cushions. The fabric is also silky smooth. These are seats intended to make the occupier feel comfortable and welcome.

Peter looks around the room. A large window behind the director stretches from floor to ceiling, encompassing the entire wall. A large cabinet and bookshelf sit on the adjacent wall, closest to Peter. The shelf is full of pictures. Most include the director shaking hands or smiling for the camera with important people. One consists of a photo of the director and Árpád Göncz, the acting president of the Republic of Hungary. Another features Director Toth with his arm around a guy Peter recognizes but can't place the name. He's the mayor of Újpest.

Finally, the director leans back, slamming the file shut. He removes his glasses and holds them in his hand, speaking to Kovacs. His voice is pleasant. Not at all what Peter had expected.

"How are things coming with the task force, Lajos?"

Kovacs had been sitting back with his arms on the armrests. Now he leans forward, rubbing his hands on his pants. "Really good. I think we just caught our first major break."

The director's eyebrows rise, but something about the movement feels unnatural. He leans back in his chair. "Oh, well, that's good news. Tell me."

Kovacs seems not to notice anything unusual, and Peter thinks maybe he's reading things wrong. Perhaps this will be a pleasant chat.

"We've taken one of the traffickers into custody. You remember the club manager?"

"Right, yes."

"Well, we found him. His name is Agoston."

"Well, that's great. I thought he'd gone into hiding. We couldn't find him."

The director's demeanor seems relaxed, but his eyes betray him.

"We were able to infiltrate a location where they were holding some of the girls they had taken. We saved eight women and captured Agoston."

Toth moves his glasses to his left hand. He turns his free hand heavenward as he speaks. "That's fantastic. I'm just surprised this is the first I'm hearing about it. I think any such operation here in

Hungary would have been brought straight to me for authorization."

Kovacs drops his eyes, speaking more quietly. "The operation wasn't in Hungary, sir. It was in Kyiv."

Toth comes forward in his chair, smashing his left hand down. The glasses break to pieces, and one of the lenses shoots off the desk, forcing both Kovacs and Peter to duck. When he speaks, his voice is furious. "How could that be, Detective? How could agents of mine be in Ukraine without my authorization?" He's leaning across his desk now, daring Kovacs to speak. His eyes are menacing.

Against his better judgment, Peter says, "Sir, it was my fault. He came because of me."

Toth turns his head, and if looks could kill, Peter would be twelve feet under. "Was I talking to you? Are you the leader of the task force?"

Unfortunately, being reprimanded by superiors is something Peter is familiar with. He knew better than to speak. Now, he follows that wisdom. He stares back at Toth.

The director turns back to Kovacs. "Now tell me, Detective. Why am I hearing about this from Interpol and the Ukrainians rather than my own agents? There must be a good explanation."

Kovacs is still looking down but finds his voice. "Sir, Peter's wrong. It was my fault. I knew Peter had gone to Ukraine from a tip he had received. I didn't even think to check with you first. I just reacted and went. I was anxious to solve the case and didn't think it through. I knew we needed to act quickly. It won't happen again."

The apology seemed to take some wind from his sails. Toth stares at him, waiting for him to raise his head before he speaks again. This time, his voice seems less angry. "I like you, Lajos. I brought Peter in on your recommendation. But I won't be made to look like a fool again. Do you understand me? I put you in charge for a reason. If any of your team, including Peter, does something like this again, I'll hold you personally responsible."

Kovacs swallows and nods.

"Now tell me about this club manager, Agoston. What do we know, and what's the plan with him?"

Chapter 39

Agoston

The room is almost entirely white. The only color is the black door and mirror on the opposite wall. Is black even a color, though? Isn't it all colors mixed together? The room has no clock or windows. I have no idea what time it is or how long they've been holding me. That's probably their plan. They want me to feel this way. Well, I'm not going to give them the satisfaction. I won't be here long.

The door opens, and a man enters. He's not the person I was expecting. He's followed by another man. I almost shot the first guy. He's Zsuzsa's boyfriend. The guy I saw flirting with her at the bar. The second guy is the one who shot me. I don't know if I'll ever be able to use my right hand again. They had a doctor look at it, but all he did was bandage it. They sit down at the table. One on either side, opposite me. Neither speaks. The shooter holds a clipboard and has a pen. He makes a note. His eyes leave the clipboard and narrow on me.

"You're in a lot of trouble, Agoston."

I'm not talking. I have nothing to say to them.

"We've got you on kidnapping, sex trafficking, and attempted murder. And that's only for starters. You're going away for a long time."

Does he think he's scaring me? He doesn't know what I know. I won't be here long. I have connections he can't even comprehend. They won't let me stay in here.

"How old are you?" he asks.

I look back at him, keeping my face blank.

He looks down at his clipboard. "Thirty-seven? I wouldn't be surprised if you get sixty years. Maybe even death. In either case, you're going to die in prison."

I can't help it; I smile at him. That's never going to happen.

"We want to help you. Cut that sentence in half. Maybe you get out when you're fifty."

I say nothing. I don't need to. Their threats are hollow.

"What do you think, Agoston? Do you want to work with us?"

I turn to the other guy, the silent one, and exaggerate a yawn. The talker looks at him. His irritation is obvious. I smile.

"You have a little brother, don't you, Agoston? József?"

This surprises me. How do they know we're brothers? József came to live with my family when he was a teenager. My mom was never his legal guardian. We have the same father but different names. Nothing links us. Nobody knows we're brothers.

"We've been holding on to him for a week. He doesn't seem so happy. Does he, Peter?"

The silent guy frowns and shakes his head, never taking his eyes off me.

"Anyway, I thought you'd want to know that since we've recovered some of the women he helped to abduct, and have more we can charge him with. He's going to stay in here almost as long as you."

Hmm. How did they link us?

"Our director told us to make every charge stick to both of you. He wants us to show no mercy. He told us not to let you speak to anyone. I get the feeling he doesn't like you two. I think he wants you to burn."

For the first time, I wonder if I've been betrayed. Abandoned.

They stand, and I place my hands on the table. My bandaged hand hurts when it bumps. "What do you want to know?"

They look at each other and sit back down.

"Who's your boss? Who's been giving you the orders?"

"I can't tell you that. If I tell you that, I'm a dead man."

The boyfriend finally speaks. "You're a dead man if you don't tell us. You live your life in prison and never get out."

"Yeah, but I'm still alive for another thirty years. If I tell you now, I don't make it past four days."

The silent one says nothing, but I can tell he's listening closely. He seems more perceptive than the talker.

"We can protect you. Nobody's listening. It's just Peter and me."

I shake my head. This guy still doesn't get it, but I can tell the silent one does.

"If I had four lives to live, I wouldn't tell you guys."

The talker starts to talk, but the silent one, Peter, cuts him off. "Well, that's your choice. We'll give you some time to think about it. Come on, Lajos. Let's go."

They stand to leave, but as they reach the door, Peter turns and walks back to me.

"Why didn't you kill Zsuzsa?" he asks.

He knows the reason. He feels the same thing for her that I do. So why is he asking?

"I've loved her for at least four years," I tell him.

He says nothing, but I can tell he gets the message.

Chapter 40

Peter

"Hi, Peter. Good to hear from you."

Peter sits at his desk in the Hungarian National Police Headquarters bullpen. It's been a long day, and he needs something to cheer his spirits. The thought of going home to an empty apartment doesn't help. He decides to call Agnes and Renata to check on them.

"Hi, Agnes, how are you? How's Renata?"

"Okay. I'm doing better than she is."

He's not surprised.

"Pretty rough for her, huh?"

"She has nightmares. She hasn't left the apartment since we got back."

Who wouldn't feel that kind of fear after enduring what she had?

"Has she been checked out by a doctor?"

"Yeah, they examined her when we got home. They said she's okay."

"What about a counselor? Someone for her to talk to?"

"They gave her a card for someone. She hasn't called her yet."

"You need to help her. Get her to call. Maybe even take her to the appointment."

"Okay."

"Agnes, she's always leaned on you. You need to help her."

"I know. I will."

"Have the two of you been more honest with each other?"

Agnes pauses. "The night we got home from Kyiv, Renata woke up from a nightmare. She was bawling, shaking like a leaf. She didn't want to be alone. We sat up talking. I told her about Dominick, and she told me about her test scores. She admitted that she's been going to school here."

"That's good to hear. She needs you, Agnes. She's been through a lot."

Peter feels the presence of someone nearby. He swivels around on his chair, looking up. Szabo and the other task force members, minus Kovacs, surround him.

"Agnes, I'm sorry, but I have to go. Say hello to Renata for me, and I'll call you soon."

Peter hangs up, turning his attention to the group. Szabo comes closer, sitting his large frame on the desk. He leans toward Peter. Peter remains in his chair, looking up at him. The other two members of the task force stay behind Peter. The behavior is not unlike a group of bullies in a schoolyard.

"You're not going to get away with it, Peter," Szabo says.

"I'm sorry. What is it I'm getting away with?"

Szabo crosses his arms. Because of the size of his belly, his arms are closer to his chest than his navel. "We know you're the leak. You're telling the traffickers about our investigation."

"How do you figure?"

"Don't try and deny it. We've all been talking, and there are just too many coincidences with you. You just happened to investigate Andras because his wife thought he was having an affair? Again, you just happen to be the one who brings in Agnes and tips us off about the club? And if that's not enough, you're the only one who knows your girlfriend was taken to Kyiv. You're the one who saved her. You've been playing us for fools, but you aren't going to get away with it any longer."

He leans toward Peter, jabbing his finger at his face, spit flying from his mouth. Peter wipes the saliva from his cheek, slides back his chair, leans away from him, and stands.

"You're right, Szabo. My investigating Andras was coincidental, but you've got the other two wrong. Agnes ran into me outside this building. She was coming to talk to anyone. And as far as Zsuzsa is concerned, she—"

"What'd you do, leave America because you were in trouble? Maybe you were trafficking there? Maybe you thought you could get away with it here." Szabo grabs Peter by the collar. "Who are you working with?"

That's the last straw. Peter considers himself rational, but when you start getting physical, that's where he draws the line. He grabs Szabo by the wrist, pulling his arm down and stepping closer to him. They're nose to nose now. "If you say one more thing accusing me of so much as a parking ticket, you won't be walking out of here under your own power."

Szabo's face colors with rage. He balls up his fist and swings at Peter. Peter sees it coming and easily sidesteps it. Szabo put so much force behind the punch he stumbles forward. Peter pushes him in the back, letting his momentum carry him forward. Szabo slides across the desk, losing his balance and falling off the other side, crashing to the ground. He screams in a fury, stumbling to his feet. Peter prepares for the charge when Kovacs steps between them.

"Stop it!" He looks at Szabo, then Peter. "That's enough."

Szabo huffs and puffs, pointing at Peter. "You're mine, Peter."

He moves forward, but Kovacs puts his hand on his chest. "That's enough, Szabo." Kovacs turns to Peter. "Take a walk."

Peter glares at Szabo, daring him to come forward. Kovacs now has his arm around Szabo holding him back.

"This isn't finished," Szabo threatens.

Peter takes his jacket off the back of his chair and walks out.

Chapter 41

Peter

Peter steps off the streetcar in Southern Buda at Móricz Zsigmond square. It's one of his favorite spots in Budapest. The cobblestone streets had once been the site of a battle between the Russians and the Hungarians during the 1956 revolution. Looking closely at some of the buildings, you can still see bullet holes in the exterior. The sun is high in the sky today, and Peter squints as he walks. Last night, snow blanketed the city, dumping four inches. White clings to the trees, occasionally breezing down with any gust of wind. It's a beautiful day, and Peter inhales the crisp air.

He's met with a chorus of laughter as he crosses the street. A group of three young teenage girls walk toward him, seemingly oblivious to him or anyone else. Peter smiles as he watches them. Their conversation makes him laugh. They all seem to be talking at the same time. Don't you need someone to be listening? As they pass, he feels a pang of heartache. The lead girl, tall and lean with big brown eyes and light curls, reminds him of Catherine.

Catherine had been his and his wife's miracle baby. After years of trying, including fertility clinics, they gave up the dream of being parents. One night, as Peter came home, he noticed a twinkle in Karen's eyes. He asked her about it, but she brushed it off, claiming it was just a good day. She took him by the hand and led him to the table, telling him to sit and wait. He could hear her singing in the kitchen as she finished preparing the meal. The smell of his favorite, chicken parmesan, wafted through the apartment.

After they ate, Peter stood to take his plate to the kitchen, but she stopped him. She told him she had something she wanted to show him and left the room. When she came back, she was holding a gift. Rarely did they ever give each other gifts outside of holidays and birthdays. Her smile at his reaction gave him pause. *What's she up to?*

"Open it," she told him.

"What's the occasion?" he asked, reaching for the gift.

"Just open it and find out."

She was so excited, and he laughed at her enthusiasm. These were the times he loved her the most. Opening the gift, he was surprised to see it was a small picture frame. He gave her a curious look, but she smiled, encouraging him to look closer. He turned it over and saw that the frame was engraved: *Fathers carry photos where their money used to be.* When he looked back up at her, he saw tears in her eyes.

"Are you..." he asked, not daring to hope.

She nodded, smiling through tears.

He stood and held her in his arms, kissing her.

That was twelve years ago, but it felt like yesterday.

As he walks through the park, he sees his friend Tom smoking a cigarette on the park bench. Since coming back to Hungary, Peter had met Tom at a screening of *O Brother Where Art Thou*. They both laughed at the same times. Some American films were dubbed with a Hungarian track. Some added subtitles. Peter preferred to see the subtitle type because he could ignore the subtitles. Tom was the same, having lived in England for several years when he was young. They became fast friends, and Peter found Tom to be a great sounding board and confidant. He gave Peter a different perspective considering he was a concentration camp survivor and retired engineer.

It takes a few seconds for Tom to see Peter.

"Well, I thought I was going to be the ugliest guy in the park today. Looks like I was wrong," Tom says, puffing out a breath of smoke.

Peter shakes his head at the old man. "I've been telling you since I met you, you need to see a different optometrist. Your reality is severely distorted."

Tom laughs, which like always, evolves into a coughing spell. Tom slides over on the bench, making room for Peter.

"What brings you over to my neck of the woods?"

"I need some advice. And it's one of those times I need you to forget this conversation immediately afterward."

"You must be really desperate. Okay, I promise."

Peter decides he needs to warm up to the conversation. "How are things? Have you seen Stephen at all?"

Stephen is a young man from America who came to Hungary for an international-business program. Stephen had hired Peter to help him find his missing girlfriend.

"I have. He seems to have settled into the country and school more. He's doing well."

"Good to hear. Odd kid, but I liked him."

Tom takes a drag from his cigarette and blows it up rather than out. "You didn't come all this way to talk about him. What really brought you?"

Peter takes a deep breath and then releases it slowly. "I think it might have been a mistake for me to take the job with the trafficking task force."

"Okay… Why do you say that?" Tom asks. He isn't even looking at Peter, instead leaning back, eyes closed, savoring his cigarette.

Peter tells him about the most recent string of girls missing from the club. About going to Kyiv and finding their location, and apprehending Agoston. About Zsuzsa and how she was taken and almost killed.

"Somebody in the task force is orchestrating this," Peter says.

"Probably, but why do you think so?"

Peter leans forward, hugging his body. It's a nice day for December but still cold.

"Kovacs crossed the border and didn't tell anyone he was coming. He had a contact with Interpol we used to infiltrate the house and apprehend Agoston. That's the only time we've been able to take someone into custody. Someone on the inside. They always seem a step ahead."

"Okay, well, let's think about this. Who's on the task force with you?"

"Kovacs, he's the team leader, then there's Szabo, Varga, and Farkas. Szabo is an arrogant prick who thinks he should be the lead on the team. I got in a fight with him before heading home last night. Varga is the only female on the team. Farkas is the youngest detective. He's a quiet guy, reserved."

"All right, let's start with Kovacs. Why might it be him?"

Peter shakes his head. "It's not him."

"Humor me for a minute. I know you don't think it's him. But why could it be him?"

"Well... he's as connected as anyone can be. He's leading the team, so if I were a trafficker, I'd want him on my side. He'd be the person I'd target."

"Okay, good. What else?"

Peter blew out his breath. "I can't think of any other reason."

"Okay, now tell me why it couldn't be him."

"He saved me when a gun was at my head in Kyiv. He invited me into the task force. He's also the only other person who knew the traffickers were in Kyiv. He could have tipped them off, but he didn't."

Tom blows out the smoke and shrugs. "Okay, how about the next one? Szabo?"

"He confronted me last night, claiming I was working with the traffickers. Anyone like that, you think maybe he's trying to deflect attention from himself. He knew about the club being investigated, and so did Varga and Farkas, for that matter, and we never apprehended anyone in there. Other than József, the pickup guy. But he was nothing. He knew even less about the operation." Peter leans back, looking up at the sky. Suddenly, he rocks forward, snapping his fingers. "Actually, there was also that strange comment in one of our briefings."

"What comment was that?"

"He implied the girls that were being taken were asking for it. That they almost deserved it because of the way they were dressed."

Tom raises an eyebrow. "Really?"

"Yes, all of us were disgusted by the comment, and he sort of backpedaled, but not completely."

A chunk of snow blows off a tree branch above, crashing at their feet. They look up, worrying more could be coming down.

Tom turns back to Peter. "Sounds like he's got the most going against him. Why isn't it him?"

This is harder, and Peter knows it's because he believed, or maybe hoped, that it was Szabo. It's no secret that he doesn't like the guy.

"Would a guilty person make the comment he did? And why did he confront me, claiming I was working with the traffickers? Seems like maybe he's grasping at straws. Frustrated, same as me."

Tom puts his arm on the bench. "Okay, and the other two, Varga and Farkas?"

"I just have a hard time seeing it being Varga. I just wouldn't think another woman would do that to these girls. Also, she seems so reserved. It could be Farkas. He seems pretty ambitious. He's young, like a lot of the traffickers. Maybe he knew them before. Neither Varga nor Farkas knew about Ukraine. If it's one of them, that could be why we actually got Agoston."

Tom throws away his cigarette and bites his lip. "Sounds like you have some work to do. Have you gotten anything out of the club manager, Agoston?"

Peter shakes his head. "Yes and no. Kovacs and I are going to try again today. We learned his brother was József, the first guy we got. We're going to try and lean on that. See if we can use it to make him talk. To this point, he's been more afraid of whoever he works for than us. But he did cryptically tell me something."

"What did he tell you?"

"I'm not sure yet, but he kept using the number four when we talked to him."

"What's the significance of the number four? What was he telling you?"

"Something I uncovered before. The key to the whole thing lies in the fourth district of Budapest."

"You know how I was in Auschwitz?"

"I think you've mentioned it every time I've talked to you. Yes, I remember."

Tom laughs. "Are you saying my conversation is predictable?"

Peter shrugs. "If the shoe fits..."

Tom shakes his head. "I don't think you deserve the wisdom. Never mind."

Peter grimaces. "Don't make me beg. What were you going to say?"

Tom pauses, then can't help himself. "One time, a fellow prisoner had stolen some food. When the Germans learned about it, they lined us up and interrogated us. When none of us would confess, they began executing us, one by one. Luckily, they started at the other end of the line. After shooting only a couple, one of my friends raised his hand and confessed. They shot him, and the executions were done. Nobody else stole food again."

Peter looks away.

"Clearly, I'm not telling you to start executing prisoners. The Nazis were devils, and they'll pay for their actions. But maybe it's time you put more pressure on this Agoston and his brother. Leave them with no choice."

Chapter 42

Peter

Peter feels anxious as he walks into the police headquarters. Szabo had attacked him last night, and that hasn't been resolved. It doesn't seem likely he'd try anything again so soon, but he seems unhinged. Anything is possible. He'll need to be careful around him.

As unsettling as that is, it doesn't compare to knowing he's working with a trafficking insider. That person, whoever he is, has the advantage. They know they're being hunted and have been for a while. They'll be on their guard now more than ever. He knows he'll need to surprise them. Do something they don't anticipate.

As he walks into the bullpen area, he sees he's not first into the office. Szabo sits at his desk, his back to him. Varga and Farkas have yet to arrive. Szabo senses his presence and turns around. When he sees who it is, his usual glare turns to ice. Peter decides to act as if nothing happened and greets him with a "Jó reggelt!" smiling broadly. Szabo rolls his eyes and looks away. When Peter reaches his desk, he sits down and looks to his right, checking Kovacs's office. The door is shut, and the light's off. That's odd. Typically he's the first one to arrive. He picks up the file on Agoston. Since leaving Tom, Agoston has been on his mind.

Inside the file, Peter finds a handwritten note:

Don't say anything, especially to Szabo, but I think we should talk with Agoston again. This time in his cell without the cameras. Something off the record. Come down and meet me at the front gates of the jail when you get in. Don't let anyone know.

Peter closes the file and stands up, walking to the bathroom. He doesn't need to go, but he also doesn't want to head straight toward the jail. Especially since it's just him and Szabo in the office. After spending a few minutes in the bathroom, he opens the door just enough to see the bullpen. Varga and Farkas have arrived, standing around shooting the breeze with Szabo. Peter leaves the bathroom and heads to the stairs. He descends two flights to the jail level. Kovacs is at the entrance waiting for him.

"Nobody saw you?"

Peter shakes his head.

Kovacs shows his credentials to the guard inside the gate.

"I'm looking for the prisoner brought in from Kyiv two days ago. Nagy Agoston."

The guard checks his list, running his finger down until it stops midway. "He's in cell forty-six. I'll take you to him. He's been held out of the general population. He doesn't leave his cell. Please sign the visitor's sheet first."

After they sign, the guard turns and walks, with Peter and Kovacs following. They reach another set of gates with another guard. The two guards greet each other as the first guard opens the gate. This time, as the gate opens, noise permeates the space. They walk across a blue metal platform that surrounds the entire jail area. There are two levels with stairs in the middle of the platform. The guard, followed by Peter and Kovacs, walks toward the stairs. After moving to the lower level, they turn to the right. Peter looks through the gate at one of the inmates in his cell. They lock eyes, and Peter feels a shiver run down his neck. The eyes can only be described as black. Hollow. Hate and anger flow from them. Peter makes a mental note not to look in any other cells.

Nobody would ever describe a jail as having a pleasant aroma. But this one seemed to get worse the farther they went. Even the guard seemed off-put by it.

"Does it normally smell like this?" Kovacs asks the guard.

The guard responds over his shoulder, "No, I don't know what's going on."

After walking halfway down the hallway, the guard stops. The ground in front of the cell has the number forty-six painted in black. Peter looks inside the cell and sees the occupant lying on the floor.

The guard slaps at the cell bars. "Hey, you've got visitors."

Agoston doesn't move.

The guard slams his keys against the cell, making a loud clanging noise.

Agoston doesn't react.

Peter and Kovacs exchange a look. The guard shoves his key into the lock, opening the cell. He enters the confined space and nudges Agoston's foot. Still, he doesn't move. It smells as if a sewer pipe has overflowed in the cell. Vomit and urine cover the floor. A food tray sits on the ground in front of the bed. Evidently, the breakfast included eggs and toast because it now litters the floor. Peter examines the body. Agoston lays ashen, unmoving. Vomit covers the mattress and floor. He's seen enough dead bodies to know one. No need to check his pulse.

"I'll go call for the doctor," the guard says and runs out of the cell.

Kovacs leans over and examines the body, holding his nose. He reaches forward and takes something from Agoston's hand. He straightens and holds it up, examining it.

"What is it?" Peter asks.

Kovacs turns around and shows him. He holds a small rock in his hand. They frown at each other, and Peter steps forward to examine the body. As he does, he notices small scratches on the concrete floor beside the hand. Peter bends down to get a closer look. Next to the hand, scratched by the rock into the floor, Peter sees *IV*. Kovacs looks at Peter, and they lock eyes before looking back down.

Chapter 43

Zsuzsa

What happened to my bar?

As I walk into the restaurant, I notice it immediately. Whiskey where the vodka should be. Off-brand labels in the front, expensive liquor in the back. I shouldn't be surprised; I've never been gone for a whole week before. Even when I'm out for a few days, I return and find things out of place. But this?

I remove my coat, hang it up, place my purse under the bar, and start working. First, I reorganize the liquor. That's what bothers me the most. Then I wipe down the bar. It doesn't have its usual shine. Gabor, the other bartender, barely wiped it at all. His laziness is irritating.

As I'm near completion, one of the cooks, Margit, sees me from the kitchen and comes in.

"Zsuzsa, you're back. We missed you."

She comes over and hugs me. She never does this. I look at her, wondering if she knows. Did Kata tell her?

"How was your vacation? Where did you go?"

"Ukraine."

"Ukraine? Why?"

It's a fair question. Why would anyone go to Ukraine in December?

"I have some family there. It's been a long time since I saw them."

She accepts that and, thankfully, doesn't ask me anything more. She returns to the kitchen, and I move on to the glasses and beer mugs. Gabor never cleans these. He runs them through the dishwasher, but that isn't enough, and I've told him so. The dishwasher leaves a film on the glass. I hate the hard water spots. I fill the sink with hot, soapy water and begin dunking glasses. Out of the corner of my eye, I see the front door open, bringing a gust of cold air.

Kata enters wearing a long red coat with big black buttons and a black fringe. Her black gloves and scarf match the coat perfectly, which is no surprise. She's the most glamorous woman I've ever known. I don't think I've seen her without perfect hair and makeup. She sees me, and instead of smiling, her brow furrows. She doesn't bother to hang her coat. Instead, she rushes to me, taking my face in her gloved hands. She looks me in the eyes, and something about that look makes me cry. I feel the tears welling up.

"Oh, honey, it's okay," Kata reassures me. "You're here now."

She takes me in her arms. I've been lying around my apartment for the last few days, recovering. When I first got home, I played my messages; at least three were from her. She was never angry in them; I had missed several shifts at work. Instead, she was worried, concerned. She cares about me. Even though I didn't want to, I dialed her number. I told her what had happened, where I had been. She didn't say much. She just sat on the other end of the phone, listening. In the end, she told me how sorry she was. She asked if there was anything she could do for me and told me not to worry about work, and to take all the time I needed.

Just three days ago, I was grateful. I didn't even want to think about work. But after a day of moping around my apartment, thinking about what had happened to me, I needed to get out. I needed to distract my mind. I needed to work. I called Kata and told her I would be in today.

After a moment more of crying in her arms, I pulled myself together and stepped away, reaching for a box of tissues under the bar.

"Honey, are you sure you're okay?" Kata asked.

"No," I admitted, laughing.

She got that concerned look in her eyes again.

"But I need to be here. I need to work."

She nods. "What does Peter say?"

"Peter? What do you mean? I haven't even heard from him since we got back."

I didn't say it to her, but that's part of why I'm crying. Who am I kidding? It's the entire reason. When I woke up in the hospital and saw him in my room, scrunched in a chair, trying to sleep, I knew he cared for me. I could see the joy in his eyes, seeing me awake. That's the second time in so many days I awoke to see his face. When Agoston had me, I was sure I would die. I had given up hope. I was barely hanging on. I wanted to die, but his face, his allure, brought me back. When I woke in the hospital bed, I wanted only him. I expected him to come to me. To kiss and hold me. That's what I wanted. But he didn't. Instead, he treated me like a porcelain doll. Like something he might hurt if he touched.

I had to get out of that hospital. I told him I wanted to go home. I got kind of pushy about it. I didn't want the concerned looks of the doctors and the nurses. I especially didn't want that from him. I thought once I was out of bed, dressed in ordinary clothes, he'd see me the way he used to. And he did. Our flight home was wonderful. I felt so safe next to him. So comfortable. I realized there was nowhere I'd rather be but with him. When we landed, and before we separated, he kissed me. Electricity shot through my body as his lips pressed against mine. I had to pull myself away from him. I sat in the taxi, leaving the curb, my eyes never drifting from his.

After arriving back at my apartment, I crashed. I slept for hours. I dreamed of him, feeling his arms around me. When I woke, I expected him to call, but he never did. I sat around my apartment for three days, praying he would call. Almost willing the phone to ring. Sometimes I found myself just staring at it. But it sat silently taunting me.

"He hasn't called?"

I shake my head.

"Oh, I'm sure it's because he wanted to give you time to rest. I'm sure he's been thinking about you."

I wipe my eyes, worrying my mascara has run.

"Well," I tell her, turning back to the glasses in the soapy water, "I'm glad to be back." I turn my head to her and force a smile. "Let's pretend none of that happened, and Peter doesn't exist. Okay?"

There's that concerned look again, but she only nods. She pats me on the shoulder and walks to her office, sensing I need time. I need to work and not think about Peter.

The rest of the day goes well. I'm amazed at how natural, and comfortable everything feels. I had worried, waking up in that hospital bed, that I would never be the same. That I would never get over it. But being back to work and keeping busy seems to be what I need. Some of my regulars come in. They welcome me back and ask where I've been. I tell them the same thing I told Margit. I went to visit family. They accept that, and I laugh and flirt with them, like always. They seem pleased to have me back.

It's getting to be later in the afternoon, and a sense of dread begins to well up. I know my shift is almost over. I don't want to go home. Margit calls out. I have some food up. I walk into the kitchen to get it, and when I return, my eyes flash to the front door. I recognize the figure immediately, the salt-and-pepper beard, the rugged shoulders. I feel my face flush, and my heart rate quickens. I pretend I don't see him. I walk over and hand my customer his food. He quips something back at me, trying to flirt, but I ignore him. It's not even intentional. From the corner of my eye, I see him taking off his long coat and walking toward me. I turn away, placing my back to him as he sits at the bar.

"Zsuzsa."

My body goes rigid. I'm now painfully aware of how I look. I brush back my hair. I wish I had known he was coming. I'm not looking my best.

"Zsuzsa," he repeats. His voice is soft, and I feel myself start to turn. How did he know I came back to work?

"Hi, Peter."

My cheeks flush again, looking into his eyes. Those eyes. The ones that drew me in from the first time they looked at me.

He hesitates. I can sense that he's drawn to me. Like I am to him. But he's reserved. Cautious. Gone is that boldness I saw outside the airport. Did I do something wrong?

"How are you doing?"

My hands are on the bar as I look at him, then past him. *Is he asking because he really wants to know? Or is that just a greeting?*

"I'm okay. How are you?"

I need to be doing something. I have to be busy. I pick up a clean glass and wash it.

"Not bad. I've been thinking about you."

I stop and look at him. He stares back at me. We're trying to see beyond the words.

"What have you been thinking?" I ask.

"I've been worried about you."

My anger flashes. "Why did it take you so long to find out?" I can see I've struck him. His mouth opens as if he wants to say something but then closes again. I can't let it go. "Is your phone broken?" He looks down. Part of me feels bad. I don't want to hurt him.

"No," he mumbles. "I thought you needed time."

He won't meet my angry gaze, and I know there's more to it than that. What's he not telling me? I decide to take it easy on him. "How about some stroganoff?"

My voice is a touch lighter now, and he can sense it. He looks up and nods, and I turn and walk back to the kitchen. What is it with this man? Why does he act like this? The tension between us is palpable, yet he's withdrawn. Why doesn't he do what I want him to do? Why doesn't he take me in his arms? His actions don't match what I see in his eyes.

I put in his order and realize I may have driven him away. I'm frustrated by him, but I want him. I want him here. I'm elated that he came. I turn and go back to the bar. As I exit the kitchen door, I hide my relief. He hasn't left. I decide I need to be nicer to him.

"Dreher?" I offer, hardly waiting for an answer.

I go to the tap, fill a mug of the dark beer, and place it before him. I check on a few of my other customers, refill some drinks, and return to him.

"There's something I haven't told you about my abduction. Something that happened that I think you need to know." He puts his beer down and rubs his beard. He's always so patient. Always preferring for me to do the talking. "I woke up and was tied to the chair, the one you found me in. Agoston was there." My hands are on the bar, but again I can't stand that. They need to be active. I pick up the towel and begin wiping the bar. "He started asking me questions. He thought I knew they were taking girls. Obviously, I did. But I didn't want him to know that."

I stop and look at Peter again. "Remember, I didn't know I was in Kyiv. I assumed they had me somewhere in Budapest. I told him that the kid in the club, the barback, was stealing alcohol from him." I start rubbing the bar again. "It worked. He started laughing and telling me I'm very unlucky. He believed that was the only thing I was suspicious of. Then another guy comes in the room and tells him that 'someone' is on the phone. Agoston leaves, and when he returns, he admits he knows you're coming to Kyiv. That you're on your way."

Peter furrows his brow. "He said *me*? He knew *I* was coming? You're sure?"

"Yes. I wouldn't forget that. I suddenly had hope."

"Then what happened?"

"They left me alone. I sat for hours with nothing to occupy my mind other than thirst. I was so thirsty. My wrists and arms hurt. I passed out from the pain."

Margit rings the bell, letting me know Peter's food is up. I serve him, top off his beer, and then check on other customers.

Over the next twenty minutes, he eats his dinner, and we don't say much. I have several other regulars who show up and seem happy to see me. Finally, I clean up his plate and bring him the bill. He lays down plenty of forints to cover the meal, leaving me a generous tip. I thank him and turn to get back to my other customers when he reaches out and grabs me by the arm, stopping me. His touch is electric. I feel like a piece of iron being pulled by a powerful magnet.

"How about a date?" he says.

"What?"

He stares into my eyes. "I'd like to take you on a date." I feel myself smile at him. "Can I take you to dinner?"

I can feel my eyes twinkling back at him. "How about Friday?" I suggest.

"I'll pick you up at your apartment at seven?"

I nod, and he turns, puts on his coat, and walks to the door. My body tingles as I watch him leave.

Chapter 44

Detective Kovacs

"Hello, Detective Kovacs."

Nemzeti Árpád, the head coroner, sits at his desk in the Hungarian National Police Headquarters' morgue. I'm not sure how he knows it's me. He has yet to look in my direction. I can see the white from his computer screen reflected in his glasses. I try to read it, squinting. But it's too small. I can't make out the words. Whatever it is, it seems to be consuming his attention.

"Hello, Árpád. How are you? How's the family?"

He has no idea I even spoke. I stand there, waiting. Finally, he looks up at me. Evidently finished with whatever he was reading.

"What?"

"I asked how your family is?"

Árpád has been married for five years. His wife, Krisztina, gave birth to twins six months ago. He put on a sizeable amount of sympathy weight during the pregnancy, probably thirty pounds. He claimed to be supporting his wife. Only she lost the weight soon after the birth. He's been gaining more. He has a big bag of chips and several cans of cola on his desk.

"If those little brats would actually sleep, I'd be a lot happier. Istvan, the boy, is pretty good most of the time, but Eszter only seems to want to sleep during the day. She's a night owl. She starts crying, Istvan starts crying, my wife starts crying, and I start crying." He laughs as he pushes back from his desk. "How are you? How's Noemi?"

"She's good. She's in her fourth year of school now. She's already smarter than me."

"Maybe she'll be something more than a detective." He laughs at his joke at my expense. I'm not sure he has much room to talk, considering he just deals with dead bodies.

"What brings you down to the crypt?" he asks.

I look down at the fast-food wrappers littering his desk. "I was wondering if you've had a chance to examine the prisoner who was found dead yesterday. The one from the jail."

"You mean the guy who died of asphyxiation?"

This was news to me. I didn't know what he had died from.

Seeing the confused look on my face, he explains. "Weren't you there when he was found? I saw your name on the witness list."

"I was. He was my prisoner. We had him on human-trafficking charges. I went there to ask him some questions."

Árpád scowls at me. "Why didn't you have him come to an interview room? Why did you go to his cell? Isn't that where he was found, in his cell?"

"I didn't want to go through the formality of having him brought up. It was a quick question. You know what kind of pain it can be to formally call up a prisoner. Who needs that paperwork?"

I could tell he wasn't buying it, but he shrugged and let it go. "I only saw him briefly. I haven't had a chance to examine him yet. But from what I saw, he died from choking on his own vomit." He turns away, waving his arm for me to follow. "He was next on my list to examine. I might as well do it now."

We reach a glass door with mirrored windows. Árpád opens the door, and I feel a whoosh of cold air. The room is colder than the rest of the office. As we enter, I see three dead bodies on separate tables. The room is small, maybe only two hundred square feet. The bodies are lined up with only about three feet between the tables. Just enough room for Árpád to squeeze between. The first body, a woman, lies with a sheet covering shoulder to ankle. Her gray, lifeless body makes me shiver.

Árpád walks past her to the next body. I recognize the colorless face of Agoston. I stop following, standing back five feet. After reaching the body, Árpád turns around to look at me. His eyes narrow. "Are you afraid of dead bodies?"

I shake my head, trying to hide the chill coursing down my back. I've seen plenty of dead bodies. But almost all of them are at the scene of a crime. They're still wearing whatever clothing they died in. For some reason, that feels more natural to me. Seeing them here, in the morgue, has a cold, eerie feeling. Árpád is watching me closely.

"Okay... afraid? No. Do I find them creepy? Yes."

He shrugs. "You'll be fine. Come over here."

He snaps on a pair of medical gloves as I reluctantly join him at the table. My head is spinning, but I force myself to concentrate.

"This is why I say he died of asphyxiation." He leans over Agoston's body, opening his mouth. Extending his index finger, he scoops his finger deep into the throat. When he brings it back out, I can see residue.

"There's his breakfast. He suffocated on his own vomit." He wipes his finger on a towel and looks at me. Now I think it might be my turn to lose my breakfast.

"The question is, why did he vomit? And why did he vomit so much that he choked on it?"

I look him in the eye, not answering.

"I have a question for you. How bad was the smell?"

"When we found him?"

"Yeah."

My stomach turns at the memory. The stench was noticeable from more than a hundred feet away. Although I hadn't recognized then that it came from his prison cell. "I bet it smelled worse than your twins filling up their diapers and being left in a warm room for an hour."

He smirks at the imagery. "That's because he was suffering from more than just vomit. He had the runs." He lifts the sheet exposing the lower half of Agoston's naked body.

"The what?"

"The runs, the squirts, the trots, tummy trouble." He rubs his belly.

"So he was throwing up and crapping his pants simultaneously?"

"Yep. Pretty unusual, right?"

"Yeah."

"That's what I thought. It could be the food in prison." He makes a face. "Not my favorite stuff. But I think it's more than that."

"More? Like what?"

"Like poison." He pauses, letting his words sink in. "Have you ever heard of the Angel Makers of Nagyrév?"

"No."

He gets a twinkle in his eye. "Back in school, I studied their case. Fascinating stuff. I never dreamed I'd see anything relevant."

"Árpád, what are you talking about?"

It's like he doesn't hear me.

"Do you know where Nagyrév is?" Before I can answer, he waves his hand. "It's a small town in western Hungary. It doesn't matter. Anyway, in this small town in 1929, there were over forty murders with thirty-four different perpetrators. Thinking about things back in 1929, it was post-World War One Europe. We had just lost a war cutting our country down by a third. Before the war, women had been subservient to their husbands. Many were forced to marry as young teenagers. During the war, husbands left, and their wives experienced self-sufficiency. They worked and had money of their own. They basked in their freedom. Many began to hope their husbands wouldn't come back. Some got lucky. Others didn't. The war ended, and the men came back. The wives were forced back into the home, losing their freedom."

He grins. "What do you think happened next?"

"The wives killed their husbands."

He gives one big clap making me jump. "Exactly! And how do you think they did it?"

"Poison?"

"Bingo!" He turns back to the corpse lying on the gurney. "And not just any poison. But a poison that makes the victim vomit and explode in their pants. Arsenic." He smiles, and I see why he works in a morgue. "I've ordered a toxicology report. I'll know tomorrow for sure."

Chapter 45

Peter

Peter has to fight his way off the subway at Nyugati Pályaudvar. He allows a pregnant woman to go before him as they exit. Once she clears the doors, people rush in. He has to muscle his way out, feeling like a salmon fighting its way upstream. Whether it's Budapest or New York City, people can't seem to wait for riders to exit.

As he clears the mass of humanity, he notices an advertisement on one of the walls. It's for a movie. He recognizes Tom Cruise on the poster. But that's not what gets his attention. It's the title of the film, *Tágra Zárt Szemek*. Translated to English, that would be *Eyes Wide Shut*. That doesn't make any sense. Could they have mistranslated it? It wouldn't be the first time. He had seen little things translated wrong since he had been back in Hungary. Maybe a song title or a news report. But a movie with Tom Cruise in it? He shakes his head. No way they translated that wrong.

As he walks up the steps from the subway station, he can't get the title out of his head—*Eyes Wide Shut*. For some reason, it resonates with him. It describes how he's feeling. Since his wife, Karen, had been murdered, he seems to be going through life with his eyes wide shut. His eyes are open, but he sees nothing. Or at least that's how it feels. Back in New York City, everything had made sense. He was great at his job, and he loved it. He had a wonderful marriage to a woman far above his punching weight. Life was good, and he felt like he had it figured out. He walked with confidence, unafraid of what might be around the corner.

When Karen was murdered, it rocked his world. Not only because he lost the love of his life, but he didn't see it coming. He had been powerless to stop it. It shook his self-confidence. That's part of why he resigned from the NYPD. He no longer believed he could do the work. Things had been a little better since coming back to Budapest. Working as a PI allowed him to focus on the cases he wanted. Those that weren't life or death if he screwed up. Then Kata came along, wanting him to investigate her husband, Andras. It was supposed to be a simple infidelity case. Instead, the guy was a human trafficker. Before Peter knew it, his life was in danger working with the National Police.

He reaches the Westend Mall. The mall opened a year ago. It rivaled anything he had seen back in the States. Big, beautiful department stores, a food court, and a fountain in the middle with large windows serving as a ceiling. It showed how far Hungary had come in the ten years since the Russians had left. Hungary was becoming Hungarian again. Coming into the food court, he searches the tables, not seeing the person he's supposed to meet, so he grabs lunch.

Since returning to Budapest, he's avoided any American fast-food options. Not that there were many. Now, looking at the Wendy's sign, he can't fight the craving for a burger, fries, and frosty. When he turns around after picking up his food, he finds Kovacs sitting at one of the tables. He walks over and sits across from him.

"Want anything?"

Kovacs shakes his head. "I'm not hungry."

Peter feels awkward now. He doesn't want to eat in front of anyone, let alone his boss.

"Don't worry about it. Just sit down and eat. I'm seriously not hungry."

Peter unwraps the burger and takes a big bite.

"I just came from the morgue," Kovacs says.

Peter's chewing on his burger and can't respond with anything other than a roll of his hand.

"Agoston was poisoned."

Peter speeds up his chewing and swallows. "Poisoned?"

Kovacs chews on his lip as he watches the people rushing around. This mall is always busy, so it surprised Peter when Kovacs suggested it. He expected somewhere more secluded.

"What do you make of it?" Peter asks.

"It's not all that surprising. We know he had information. The question is, what's that information, and who killed him."

That's exactly what Peter had been thinking. They sit there, lost in their own thoughts.

Finally, Kovacs breaks the silence. "I think it goes without saying, but we can't trust anyone at this point. Everything must be kept between us until we know who the killer is. I'll try and find out who had access to the inmate's breakfast. Why don't you start looking into the other task force members."

"You know they hate me, right? Especially Szabo."

"Maybe it's about time you start trying to win them over, become their friend."

Peter takes a big spoonful of his frosty. "Or maybe draw out the guilty one?"

"How would you do that?"

"Make them believe the truth is about to come out. See if the guilty one takes the bait."

Chapter 46

Peter

Peter looks down at his watch as he sits in the small conference room of the Hungarian National Police Headquarters. It's five minutes after four p.m., and Szabo still hasn't come. It's not like him to be late, especially with his desk only thirty steps away. Peter starts to accept the idea he isn't coming. That isn't anything surprising. It's no secret he doesn't like or trust Peter. He had accused him of being a trafficker and killer. Those are strong cues of distaste. Then he had confronted Peter and tried to fight him. Those actions cement the idea Peter won't be receiving any Christmas cards from the Szabo family.

But Peter knows he needs Szabo. He's the key to his plan. Szabo has made it clear to everyone who knows him that he can't help but open his big mouth. He loves to talk, and he loves to gossip. Peter plans to exploit that weakness. But if Szabo won't meet and play along, Peter will have to reimagine the whole plan.

Looking down at his watch again, he knows it's time to give up. It's now fifteen after the hour. Standing up from the table, his mind has already moved on. He considers a plan B. That's when he hears a set of heavy footsteps tromping outside the door. Peter sits back down.

The door opens, and Szabo steps inside, slinging daggers at Peter with his eyes. He doesn't sit or close the door. "What's this about, Peter?"

"Thanks for coming to see me, Szabo. Shut the door, and have a seat. It'll only take five minutes of your time."

Szabo closes the door, but he doesn't sit down. He does take a few steps toward the table.

"I know you and I haven't seen eye to eye on several things, but I hope you'll hear me out. I have something important to discuss with you."

Szabo's eyebrows raise, and he pulls out a chair, sitting at the table across from Peter.

"I've decided to leave the task force."

Szabo gives him a sideways look. Mistrust is evident on his face. "Why?"

"I'm just not cut out for this. It's so much different than New York City. I thought I could handle it, but I can't. I came back to Budapest to investigate smaller crimes. This is too much for me. My life's been in danger a couple of times."

"Just like that? You quit."

Peter hesitates, seemingly conflicted. "Well... honestly, it's not just that. There's more."

Szabo tries to act disinterested, leaning back in his chair. "What else?"

"I don't trust our team."

Szabo chuckles, shaking his head. "No, Peter, we don't trust *you*."

Peter holds up his hands. "I'm not pointing my finger at you or any other team member. It's the leadership I don't trust."

Szabo's eyes narrow. "What do you mean by that?"

"I think our team is fractured because of the leader."

"Kovacs?"

"Exactly. Teams perform only as well as leaders lead. I don't think he's leading. I think you should be in charge."

Szabo furrows his brow, puffing out his chest. "I thought you and Kovacs were close?"

"We are... I mean, we have been." Peter drops his voice to a whisper. "But I just learned something about him."

Szabo leans closer, matching Peter's tone. "What was it?"

Peter steals a glance back out the window toward the bullpen. Szabo also turns to look.

"Does it seem like he's withholding information? Like he's not sharing everything with the whole task force?"

Szabo leans back, chuckling again. "You mean like the two of you going to Ukraine and not telling the rest of us about it? Like that?"

Peter can't hide the exasperation in his voice. "Yes, like that... and other things."

"What other things?"

Peter hesitates, seemingly unsure whether he should say more.

Szabo's eyes narrow. "What, Peter? Tell me."

Peter leans even closer, his voice barely above a whisper. "Somebody poisoned the club manager, Agoston, and Kovacs knows who it is."

Szabo presses his lips together, then brings his hand up to rub his cheek.

"Kovacs is going to expose whoever it is. He has some kind of evidence locked away in his office."

Szabo looks at Peter warily. "How do you know this?"

"I overheard him talking to the doctor in the morgue."

"Árpád?"

Peter snaps his fingers and points at him. "Yep, him."

"Well, that means Árpád knows also."

Peter shakes his head. "No, I distinctly heard Kovacs tell Árpád he wants the test results from the toxicology report to go to him. Nobody else. He said it was imperative that nobody else knows. He even forbade Árpád from looking at it."

"So what's in the toxicology report?"

"I don't know, but Árpád told Kovacs he'd deliver it to his office tomorrow morning. Kovacs will see the results when he gets into the office around eight. He'll know then who's working with the traffickers."

"I don't understand how a toxicology report will show anything other than if Agoston was poisoned?"

Peter shrugs. "I don't either. But Kovacs seems convinced. That's why I believe he's withholding more information. He's not telling us everything but expects us to do a good job. That's not an environment I want to be in. That's why I want to go back to private investigation."

"Why are you telling me this?"

"The other members of the team trust you. They listen to you. And I think you should be the leader."

Szabo straightens in his chair, puffing out his chest. He leans over and slaps Peter on the shoulder. "Sorry to see you go, but thanks for telling me."

"I won't go yet. Not until this has been resolved. But I'm not going to be here long, and I thought you should know."

Chapter 47

Detective Kovacs

It's still dark, but I know I'm not getting any more sleep tonight. Typically, I'm comatose as soon as my head hits the pillow. A bomb could go off in my room, and I wouldn't know it. Nadia used to get so frustrated with me when Noemi was a baby. Noemi would cry, and I wouldn't hear her. Nadia would begin by elbowing me. Then she'd kick me. Finally, she'd give up and go get her. She'd bring her into the bed with us, and I wouldn't know it until I woke up.

But not tonight. Tonight I stare at the ceiling, listening to Nadia's rhythmic breathing. As I turn my head, I can barely make out the shape of her face in the darkness. I'm jealous. She sleeps like she doesn't have a care in the world. Our life together hasn't been without its trouble. Some of that's been money. No, who am I kidding? Most of it's about money, or the lack thereof. We were never destined to be rich, Nadia a bookkeeper in an accounting office, me a police officer-turned-detective. But we got by. Things were tight but comfortable until Noemi was born.

We were so excited when we learned we would be parents. Nadia had an ideal pregnancy, other than a slip on the ice when she was six months pregnant. The day she went into labor was both exciting and scary. Everything looked good for the first few hours, but then she stopped progressing. For hours she fought contractions without any progress. Finally, after almost two days of labor, the baby's blood pressure dropped significantly, and they worried she might not survive the delivery. The doctor used forceps to force the delivery. I can still picture the doctor's concern when Noemi delivered. To the casual observer, she looked like an ordinary, healthy baby girl. But watching her for any length of time, you saw that her lower body never moved. She would cry and wiggle her little arms, but never the legs. She was examined and reexamined with little explanation of what was wrong. Finally, a specialist confirmed what we had feared: our little girl would never walk or have the use of her legs. A scan confirmed the problem in her spinal cord. The specialist was noncommittal about whether it was due to injury or development. Nadia and I had cried for our little girl, knowing she'd never have an everyday life. You don't realize how many things require working legs until you don't have them.

I no longer hear the deep breathing next to me as I turn my head back to Nadia.

"Are you awake?" she whispers.

"I am."

"Why?"

The life of a detective is hard. The life of a detective's wife might be worse. Not only do you have to wait up nights, unsure if your husband will come home, but on those long nights, you may never get the full story of why. At least, that's how our relationship is. I never want to bring my work home with me. Which means I'm also closed off to any detail when she asks. I opt to tell her only enough to end the questions.

"I'm thinking about the case I'm working on right now."

She leans up on an elbow, the concern evident in her moonlight eyes. "What case?"

"Oh... I had a witness who was murdered in the jail."

"Who murdered him?"

"I don't know. That's what has me stumped."

She leans down to me, snuggling below my armpit, resting her head on my chest. "Anything I can do?"

I smile at her hair. "Cast a spell and put me back to sleep?"

Her hand rubs at my T-shirt. "I can't promise you that... but I can try and wear you out."

I hear the flirtation in her voice more than I can see it.

I feel her hand run under my shirt as she climbs on me, straddling me.

Nagy Árpád sits behind his desk as I walk into the morgue. He holds a pastry in his hand; another is on the desk in front of him. A large cup of coffee sits beside it. He looks up and sees me, takes a big bite, then stands and wipes his hands on his white coat.

"I have your results for you," he mumbles with a full mouth.

That's what I had hoped.

"What are you doing here so early?" I ask.

He chuckles. "It was either come here or stay home with two crying babies."

"So you left your wife by herself with two unhappy babies?"

"No." He shrugs. "My mother-in-law came over."

I try to keep judgment out of my voice as I ask, "Okay... what do you got?"

He reaches over his pastry, coffee, and the pile of files littering his desk. He hands me a folded sheet.

I take it from him, looking him in the eye. "Nobody else has seen this?"

"Nobody."

As I look at the form, I notice the deceased name, date of birth, location, etc. My eyes roam lower to the line indicating what was found in the bloodstream at the time of death. Several items were listed, but I was only concerned with one. I look back up at Árpád.

"Just as I told you, he died of arsenic poising."

"Do you have an envelope?"

Árpád gives me a curious look but reaches back into a filing cabinet and withdraws a box of envelopes. He hands one to me, and I stuff the report in, sealing the lip.

"Will you do me a favor and write my name on the outside?"

He raises an eyebrow but takes the envelope from me, scribbling my name on the outside and handing it back. I thank him and head for the door when a thought hits me.

"How would you obtain arsenic?"

He shrugs. "It's pretty easy to get. It's in loads of things."

"For example?"

He looks up at the ceiling. "It's in all kinds of food—shellfish, mushrooms, poultry, even vegetables. Arsenic is a common material found on the earth's surface. Many countries have groundwater contaminated by it. Tobacco can even have arsenic because of the water used to irrigate it."

"So he could have been poisoned by the food? It could have been an accident?"

"It could have been. But for that high a level in his bloodstream, I doubt it. He'd have to have horrible luck. One in a million. Several things would have had to happen. And nobody else seems to have that problem in the jail, right? I haven't seen any other bodies in here."

He had a point.

"How else might he have been exposed to it?"

"Arsenic has a lot of industrial uses. It's used as an alloying agent. It's also used in processing glass, pigments, textiles, paper, metal adhesives, and ammunition. High levels of arsenic are also in pesticides and rat poisons. It's all around us."

I thank him again and head out the door.

The National Police Headquarters is never closed, but this morning it seems like it. The night shift of employees is much smaller than the group working during the day. I head back upstairs toward my office, but I have no intention of going inside. In the foyer, I find who I'm looking for. József, the night security guard, is sitting behind a lobby desk, reading the newspaper. He looks up with surprise as he hears me coming. Sound carries on the marble floors.

"You're in early."

"Yeah, too much on my mind right now. Could you do me a favor? Will you go and place this on my desk?"

He takes it from me, but I know what he's thinking. If I were him, I'd think the same thing. I feel like I need to justify the request.

"I have to go down to the jail and don't want to take it with me."

He shrugs. "Okay."

He sets it down on the table in front of him.

"I need it there right away."

He looks up at me, and although he tries to hide it, I can see fire in his eyes. He stands, picks up the envelope, and heads toward my office.

I call out my thanks to his back as he walks, but he doesn't acknowledge it. I head off, walking to the jail. It's not far, just down the hall and a short elevator ride. As I reach the doors, right before the metal detectors, the two guards look up at me with surprise.

"Do you guys have the log of visitors for the last few days?"

One with a too-tight uniform tells me there is a different log for each day. I tell him I want to see the one from two days ago. He goes into their little office, comes out holding two sheets of paper, and hands them to me. I take them and read down the list. It surprises me how many names are on it. This isn't a big jail. Mainly used for those recently arrested but not yet arraigned. Turning the sheets, I review each name. None are names I'm looking for.

"Can I see the log from three days ago?"

He takes the sheets from me, goes back into his little office, then comes back with a new sheet. He hands it to me, and I scroll down the list. Again, I don't see any names I expect. Just as I'm about to give it back to him, a name gives me pause. That's odd. I can't figure out why that name would be on the list.

I give him back the sheet, thank him, and head out the doors.

Chapter 48

Peter

Peter enters the doors of the National Police Head Quarters at 8:01 a.m. He had planned to arrive at least twenty minutes earlier, but nothing seemed to be going as expected. He got out of bed five minutes late, dropped his teacup, which shattered into a million pieces, and missed the streetcar as it pulled out. He hopes that doesn't indicate what the rest of the day has in store.

He had planned to arrive early to keep a watchful eye on Kovacs's office. Unfortunately, someone could have already come, taken, or at least read the report, then left without Kovacs or Peter knowing. As Peter steps into the task-force bullpen, he takes a different route than usual to his desk. He walks around the perimeter, making sure to pass Kovacs's office. As he passes, he looks through the window seeing the envelope sitting on his desk, untouched.

As he hangs up his coat and sets down his briefcase, he looks around the room. Szabo, Varga, and Farkas are all there. They've beaten him in this morning. Only Kovacs is missing. Szabo, uncharacteristically, nods a good morning to him. Varga smiles and waves, and Farkas doesn't seem to notice him. This is the first morning he actually feels welcome.

A few minutes later, Varga comes over.

"We might have a lead on where the traffickers have moved their operations."

"Oh yeah?"

She wears a conservative navy-blue skirt and jacket with a floral-print blouse. He doesn't find her attractive; she's not his type. But he can see how many would. Especially dressed as she is today. He also likes how she's wearing her hair, pulled back with a bow, matching the blouse.

"Another club."

She drops a file on Peter's desk and walks away. He watches her as she leaves, expecting her to return to her desk, but instead, she heads toward Kovacs's office. She has another paper in her hand. Peter watches closely as she enters the office, but she simply puts the report on his desk and walks out. Never touching or looking at the envelope.

Peter turns to the file. Opening it, he takes note of the club's name, Szerelmes. The word means *love* in Hungarian. If this is the club where the traffickers are now operating, many girls will find anything but by going inside. He opens the file and finds a picture of a girl, pretty with dark hair and large eyes. Her name is Sandor Judit. He scans the page, reading about her.

She was last seen on December 14, nine days ago. That would mean she went missing the same day as Renata. But she wasn't one of the girls found in Ukraine. She's still missing. His eyes scan lower on the page. She wasn't reported missing until December 20. Hmm... six days is a long time for someone to be missing before being reported, especially a girl of her age, only sixteen. He scans further down the page and finds she's one of two children in her family. She's the oldest, with a ten-year-old sister. No father, and her mother works two jobs. None of that is particularly unusual. Plenty of single mothers are in the city fighting to provide for a family. The next piece of information gets his full attention. She was not reported missing by her family. Her mom never reported it. A classmate reported it when she stopped coming to school.

Peter leans back in his chair, continuing to stare into the eyes of the missing girl. Why wouldn't her family have reported her? Did her mother think she ran away from home? But even if she did, why wouldn't she report her as a runaway? Something feels wrong about this. Peter looks up and stares at each task force member. Why are they sure this is connected?

Peter returns to the file. With the mother working two jobs and Judit being in school, they probably hardly saw each other. Peter looks at their home address, Nádor u. 1a in Budapest. He grabs a map of Budapest. The term "map" doesn't do it justice. It's way more than that. The spiral-bound book has the entire city indexed and addressed. He shuffles to the back, looking for Nádor Street. Finding it, he flips back to the map. The map is of Újpest, the fourth district.

Peter leans back in his chair and crosses his arms. Agoston, before he died, wrote *I V* on the ground. At first, he believed Agoston was trying to say something about himself. Something in English that Peter would pick up on. I something... Now he realizes it was a location. He was referencing the fourth district of Budapest, Roman numerals IV. Peter has another thought. He looks in the map book again, this time finding the address for the Szerelmes. Seeing it in the back and then flipping to the map, he knows before he looks—"Szerelmes" is also in Újpest.

Peter stands from his desk. He needs to walk. His head is spinning with possibilities. *What does this mean*? Renata was also taken in Újpest. But what if this abduction isn't related? The girl wasn't found among the others. She's still missing but taken the same day. Plus, all of the girls taken before by Andras were from places outside of Budapest. Almost none were local. This girl grew up in Budapest. In Újpest, no less. He isn't sure why, but he knows he has just found something significant.

He walks to the bathroom. After a quick trip, he passes by Kovacs's desk again. The envelope still sits on his desk, unchanged. But, as Peter returns to his own desk, he's surprised to see an envelope sitting on it. He sits and opens it. The writing is large, in block letters:

STOP INVESTIGATING AND LEAVE THE TASK FORCE IMMEDIATELY, OR SOMEONE YOU CARE ABOUT WILL DIE

He looks up and surveys the room. Szabo, Varga, and Farkas still sit at their desks. None of them are looking at him. Szabo seems to be enthralled by whatever he's reading. Varga is typing on a computer, and Farkas is talking on the phone.

Peter stands and walks to Varga. She stops typing and looks up.

He holds up the file in his hand. "Why do you think this girl was taken by the traffickers? I don't see anything in the file to suggest that."

She shrugs. "Szabo told me that. And she's about the same age as Renata."

Peter nods and walks back to his desk.

Chapter 49

Peter

Peter feels a rush of exhilaration as he opens the outside door to the Hungarian National Police Headquarters. That exhilaration is only mildly dampened by the arctic blast that hits him as the external air cuts through his clothing. It's now 10:05 a.m., and he had made plans to meet Kovacs at ten-thirty. He couldn't wait to share what he had learned with him. And tell him about the note.

Peter heads to the subway stop at Göncz Árpád City Center. It takes five minutes for the subway to arrive and another ten minutes until he reaches his stop, Nyugati Pályaudvar. The subway is quiet, and it gives him time to think. Beyond his excitement about finally having a solid lead about the mole, he also feels relief. He's harbored fears Kovacs could be the insider. Those fears never seemed justified. But he knew it would be naïve to not suspect everyone. The note on his desk confirmed Kovacs's innocence. No way Kovacs could have delivered it. He had grown close to Kovacs. Learning he was involved in the trafficking would have crushed him. If he feels alone now, imagine what he might feel like without Kovacs as his ally.

Reaching Nyugati Pályaudvar, Peter exits the train. Climbing the stairs, he feels the chill of the air. He squints against the sun's powerful rays. It's a clear, chilly, blustery day in Budapest. Peter walks a couple of blocks until he reaches Margit Bridge. The bridge is described as a three-way bridge because it links Buda to Pest and Margit Island, a small island on the Danube River. The bridge is the second-oldest bridge in the city, having been constructed in the 1870s. Only the Chain Bridge is older. What's unique about this bridge is the middle. One can walk down a set of stairs from the bridge to access the island. Peter had suggested this spot when he and Kovacs discussed a meeting place for today. Peter always preferred meeting outside, no matter the time of year. What he neglected to consider was the wind that might come up. Being in the middle of the bridge, nothing blocks airflow. The wind could be strong, and with the already chilly weather, neither would want to stay long.

Peter walks until he reaches the middle of the bridge, hugging himself against the cold. Once he reaches the designated spot, he stands and looks south, admiring the view. On the Buda side, he can see the Castle District, Matthews Church, Fisherman's Bastion, and Gellert Hill in the distance. As his gaze moves east to the river, he can see the Chain Bridge and the Elizabeth Bridge. Bringing his gaze back to Pest, he can see the vast parliament building at the side of the river. He never seems to tire of the city sights. Behind him, he hears the chime of the streetcar as it approaches. The wide bridge allows cars to drive in either direction, with a streetcar track running down the middle. Pedestrian sidewalks line either side along the edges.

He looks down at his watch: ten-thirty. The streetcar stops, and several riders exit. Peter recognizes the big frame of Detective Lajos Kovacs. He must have seen Peter from the streetcar window because he never looks up. Instead, he walks straight to him.

As he approaches, Peter smiles. "Glad to see you made it."

"Yeah, I almost didn't. Couldn't you have picked somewhere inside? It's freezing."

Peter nods. "At least you were smart enough to ride the streetcar. I walked."

Kovacs shakes his head and turns to look at the river, leaning against the bridge railing.

"I've got some good news. Or maybe I should say *some* news," Peter says.

Kovacs nods and looks at Peter with intense eyes. "You aren't the only one. But go ahead and tell me what you have first."

"Do you remember the *I V* on the floor of Agoston's cell?"

Kovacs furrows his brow. "I do."

"I think I know what he was trying to tell us."

"Tell me."

"The key to this investigation is Újpest. Whoever's behind it is either from Újpest or lives there now. Or maybe they're operating from there. But Újpest is the key."

"Yeah, I came to the same conclusion. At least, that lines up with what I learned."

Kovacs says something else, but Peter can't hear it. A screech of tires beside them drowns his words. A car jumps the curb and heads right at them. Peter lurches to the right while Kovacs goes left. The car narrowly misses Peter but strikes Kovacs at the waist pressing him into the bridge's railing. Peter's eyes are transfixed on his friend. Kovacs screams in agony. His face has gone white. The car breaks through the barrier, and Peter watches in horror as Kovacs's body is severed in two at the waist. His upper half flips in the air toward the cold, dirty water. The car follows behind him. Peter rushes to the ledge looking down as his friend hits the water. A large splash emanates from the strike point, rising toward Peter. Within seconds, Kovacs and the car are submerged. Peter feels his knees give way as he slumps to the ground. He's barely aware of the people rushing toward him.

Chapter 50

Peter

Peter sits clutching a hot teacup, trying to warm himself. After watching the pain and agony on his friend's face as he fell to his death, an ambulance came to take Peter to the local hospital. After being examined by a doctor and treated for shock, he was moved to a recovery room. Sitting wrapped in a blanket and sipping a hot tea, he finds time to reflect. *Had that been accidental? Who had been driving the car? Was Kovacs the target? Or was I? Did the driver remain in the car, or had he exited prior to impact?*

Too many questions with no answers. Peter looks up as the door to the hospital room opens, and a nurse steps inside.

"I'm sorry to disturb you, but I need to retake your blood pressure."

She pulls back his blanket and rolls up his sleeve. She places the cuff around his bicep and squeezes the air bulb. She's watching him closely, and Peter gets the feeling this is more than a measurement of his blood pressure. Finally, she releases the valve, and the squeezing he felt in his arm subsides.

"That's much better. The doctor was concerned with your blood pressure when you first came in, but now it's normal." She looks into his eyes, studying them. "How are you feeling?"

How does someone answer that? He had just witnessed the murder of his friend and boss. In many ways, the only person he could truly rely on. And he might have been the actual target, not Kovacs.

"I'm okay, considering."

The nurse continues to search his eyes. He sees warmth there. "Well, since your blood pressure has fallen, and you were uninjured in the accident, you're free to leave. The doctor has already signed for your release. Also, you have a visitor outside."

Peter stands, thanks her, and extends the teacup.

She waves at him. "Just have it. You aren't done yet, and I want to ensure you warm up. The hospital has plenty of teacups."

As he walks into the hallway, he's surprised to see who's waiting for him.

"How are you feeling?" Szabo asks.

"I've been better."

Szabo looks down as they walk toward the elevator. "I know it's recent, but I need to ask you a few questions."

Peter looks at him as he calls the elevator. Szabo stares back. His eyes are cold. He sees none of the sympathies he saw in the nurse's eyes.

"Ask your questions."

The elevator arrives, and they step inside.

"What were you doing there?"

"Kovacs and I were there to talk."

"About what?"

This is a tricky question to answer, especially to someone Peter can't trust. He's also very aware now that Szabo knows he was lying about not trusting Kovacs.

"We were meeting to talk about what I told you yesterday. About me leaving the task force."

The elevator reaches the bottom floor, and they step off.

"What was Kovacs's reaction?"

"I hadn't told him yet. We'd just arrived."

"Why didn't you meet in our offices? Why the secret meeting on the bridge?"

Peter doesn't have a good answer for this.

"I told him I'd rather not meet in the office. Given everything that's happened, I didn't know who would be listening."

Szabo has to step around a group of doctors and nurses pushing a patient on a gurney.

"So it was your idea to meet on the bridge?"

Peter knows where this is going but sees no way around it.

"Yes."

They reach the hospital's front doors, and Szabo indicates Peter should accompany him to his car. Peter complies, walking over to the black Volkswagen Passat. After getting seated, Szabo starts the car and says, "So, walk me through it. Tell me about what happened."

Peter talks as Szabo drives. He tells him about leaving the office, riding the subway, walking onto the bridge, and feeling the cold. About arriving at the designated spot, seeing Kovacs exit the streetcar, and walking up to him.

"Did you notice anyone following you?"

"No."

"Even on the subway?"

"No."

"Did you notice anyone else on the bridge? Anyone who might have followed Kovacs?"

"No."

"Tell me about the accident. What did you see?"

"I didn't see much. While we were talking, I heard a screeching noise behind me. When I turned, I saw a car barreling toward us."

"What kind of car?"

"A sedan. I'm not sure what kind. It happened so fast."

"What color?"

"Dark... Black or maybe dark blue." Peter decides it's his turn to ask a question. "Did you recover the car?"

Szabo honks his horn at the car in front of them. The light's turned green, but the car isn't moving. The momentary pause in conversation gives Peter a chance to consider. This might be a first for him. He's never been interrogated by the person who might actually be the killer.

"We did. We also recovered Kovacs's body. At least, what's left of it."

"What about the driver?"

Szabo shakes his head. "Disappeared without a trace." He looks away from the road and into Peter's eyes. "Did you notice anything about the driver?"

Szabo turns the wheel, and Peter thinks back to the scene. It all happened so fast. It's a blur. He looks out the window and notices they're headed toward his apartment, not back to headquarters.

"Not really, no."

"Not really? Or not at all?"

"Not at all. I was too shocked. My eyes were on Kovacs once he got hit."

"Anything else you remember?"

They pull up to Peter's apartment building. Szabo puts the car in neutral and takes his foot off the clutch turning to Peter.

Peter shakes his head.

"You're off for the rest of the day. Go ahead and relax. I'll call you after Christmas. Just keep your phone on and stay available."

Peter nods and moves to get out of the car, but Szabo grabs his arm before he can exit.

"And Peter, one more thing. It's not lost on me that you said you couldn't trust Kovacs just yesterday, and now he's dead. You were the last person to see him alive. You suggested the spot to meet. Like everyone else in your life, they get too close to you and end up dead. You're a suspect as much as anyone else. Don't go anywhere. Stay available."

Chapter 51
Director Toth

I hear the doorbell buzz as I press the button on the gate at the front of the house. I've never been here before, although I've spoken with Kovacs many times when he was at home. It's a small, lovely home, nestled in the Buda hills, away from the hustle and bustle of downtown. The house is maybe ten years old. It has an orange tile roof and a yellow plaster exterior. There's no garage, but it has a small driveway with a closed gate. You can enter the house either from the side by the driveway or via the front door. Extending from the porch is a sidewalk that leads to the gate.

This is a meeting I've been dreading. I've met Kovacs's wife, Nadia, several times. Mostly at social functions. I'm not even sure I'd recognize her if I met her on the streets. I hear the side door open, the one closest to the road. I can't see her, but I hear her calling out that she's coming. "Jövök. Jövök." Her tone sounds chipper and upbeat.

She comes around the corner of the house and sees me. All that's visible behind the wooden gate is my head. I can see recognition hasn't dawned yet. She looks at me curiously. Probably thinks I'm here to sell something. As she grows closer, I can see that she now recognizes me. Her eyes narrow, and she increases her pace. She reaches the front gate as I wave and smile. She frowns, waving back. She opens the gate.

"Director Toth?"

"Hello, Nadia."

She stands there awkwardly, unsure if she should invite me in.

"Can I help you?" she asks.

I motion toward the house. "Can I come inside for a few minutes?"

She frowns. A line creases the center of her forehead. "Of course." She bids me to follow her. I walk along the sidewalk and up the steps reviewing what I might say to her as we make our way inside. As the director, I've had to make similar visits a few times. This would be different, because as of now, we don't know who the killer is.

After opening the front door, we enter the house, and she leads me to the small kitchen table. Four chairs would fit, but this table only has three. It's obvious where their daughter, Noemi, would fit. I take a seat.

"Can I get you anything? Juice? Soda? Water?"

"No, I'm fine. Thank you."

She occupies one of the chairs across from me. "I don't have much time." She looks across the room at the clock on the wall. "I need to leave soon to pick up Noemi."

I've already sent a uniformed police officer to pick up Noemi, but she doesn't know that.

"Nadia," I start, "I have some difficult news."

Her lower lip trembles, and she raises her hand to her face. She must have been expecting this since finding me outside her home.

"Lajos was involved in an accident today."

Her eyes look right through me. "How bad?"

I shake my head and look down, unable to meet her eyes. "He was killed."

Her hand shakes as she lets out a moan. Tears roll down her cheeks. She holds her hand to her mouth. Agony is written across her face.

"I'm sorry."

She drops her head in her hands. Her body is racked with sobs. I feel powerless to provide any comfort.

Chapter 52

Peter

"I thought I might find you here."

When Peter enters the park, he's happy to see the bench occupied by his friend. It's late in the afternoon, and shadows extend east from the buildings. Within twenty minutes, the sun's rays will be completely gone. But for now, the bench is still nestled in the warmth of the sun. Tom makes use of the remaining sunlight, smoking a cigarette.

"What brings you here?" he asks Peter.

Peter takes a seat next to him as Tom scoots over.

"I came to see you."

"Why would anyone do that?" Tom smiles.

"I needed someone to talk to. And you seemed like my best option."

Peter doesn't add that he's now one of his only options.

"I feel sorry for you."

Tom takes a drag on his cigarette.

Peter isn't sure how to say any of his thoughts, so they come out in a rush. He tells Tom about the latest developments in the trafficking case. About the club manager being poisoned, Kovacs's death, and how he and Kovacs were closing in on the puppet master in the police. Tom, in his usual way, says nothing. Puffing away on his cigarette, listening.

When Peter finishes, Tom looks him in the eye. "So, who do you think is pulling the strings?"

Peter looks back at him. "I think it's the director."

"Toth."

Peter nods.

"Why do you think that?"

Peter tells him about his interrogation of Agoston, the club manager. About how he wrote *I V* on the floor of the jail cell. "I think he felt betrayed by Toth and wanted to let us know. When I was in Toth's office, I saw a photo of him shaking hands with the mayor of Újpest. I did some research and learned Toth grew up there. He and the mayor are close friends. Also, all of the girls who were taken were from outside Budapest. A recent victim came from district four. That can't be a coincidence. Agoston was telling us she's the key."

Tom's eyes narrow, but he says nothing.

"Both clubs are in Újpest. Toth has the clout and position to cover his tracks."

"Why would he do this? He's already a powerful man. What incentive would he have?"

It's a good question and something Peter doesn't have an answer for.

"So all this time, you've been working for the man orchestrating the trafficking?"

"It would appear that way."

Tom makes a "humph" sound. They sit thinking of the ramifications.

"Do you have any proof?"

Peter looks at him shaking his head.

"I've got to go check into this girl from Újpest. There had to be a reason for her to disappear. She's the right age for the trafficking, but nothing else about it makes sense. She's also still missing. She hasn't been found."

"Like what? What about her doesn't make sense?"

"I already told you she's from Budapest, and the others aren't."

"Yeah. So? There might be other missing girls from Budapest. What's significant about her?"

"She was reported missing six days after she was last seen. That's too long for a girl with a mother and another sibling. She lived with her family. They knew she was gone but didn't report it. Why?"

Tom shrugs. "You tell me."

"That's what I have to find out. I need to talk to the mother."

Tom tosses away his cigarette. "Why do you think it took you so long to see this? About the director, I mean."

Peter had been asking himself the same question. "I'm not sure. He's been on my list of suspects for a long time. I just couldn't understand why he'd do it. I still don't."

Tom leans his head to the side. Peter can see he has another thought but seems hesitant to bring it up.

"What?"

"Do you think this has happened to you before?"

Peter isn't sure what he means by that.

"I mean, did you miss something in the past because you didn't suspect the man in charge? Maybe the boss didn't figure into your list of subjects."

Peter frowns. "You mean with my wife?"

Tom nods.

"Yes, it's been bouncing around my head a lot. Whenever I see Toth, I think of my boss, the NYPC commissioner. After Karen was killed, I was in shock. I never thought it could be someone I worked with. I assumed it was someone I'd put away, and they were looking for revenge. Believe me. This has made me see Karen's case in a whole new light."

Tom nods. They fall into silence before Tom says, "What about Zsuzsa?"

"What about her?"

"Have you seen her since Ukraine?"

With all the excitement of the last couple of days, Peter isn't sure what day it is. He's got a scheduled date with her coming up.

"What day is it?"

"Friday."

Peter puts his head in his hands. "I forgot. I'm supposed to go out with her tonight."

Tom frowns. "You don't look so happy about that."

Peter grimaces. "It's not that. It's just... I don't know how good a company I'll be. I've got a lot on my mind and feel pretty exhausted."

Tom pats him on the shoulder. "What time are you supposed to pick her up?"

Peter looks at his watch. "Seven, but maybe I can call her."

"Why? It's only four-thirty. You have plenty of time."

"Maybe I can call her and reschedule for another night."

Tom shakes his head. "You don't deserve her."

Peter stares at him.

"I'm sorry, but you don't."

"Why?"

"Because from the sounds of it, she's out of your league anyway. Plus, she helps you solve multiple cases, including putting herself in danger. And she patiently waits for you to ask her out again. If you don't go tonight, just do the girl a favor and leave her alone."

Peter feels a flash of anger. How dare he say that. He doesn't understand all Peter's been through over the last week.

"I'm sorry, Peter, but it's true. You've been an idiot with her. I can say this to you because I'm your friend."

Peter's about to respond and justify his actions, but he knows Tom's right. He doesn't deserve Zsuzsa.

Seeming to read his thoughts, Tom has one more piece of advice. "And Peter, stop seeing a date with a beautiful woman as an obligation. You need her more than she needs you."

Peter frowns. He's not seeing her as an obligation.

"Oh, stop it. I say that to you because I care about you. You need her. You don't realize the hole you have in your life. She can change your life for the better. Go to her and give her a chance. Stop wallowing in self-pity. Stop feeling guilty for caring about Zsuzsa. Let yourself love her."

Peter looks away from Tom and stares up at the leafless trees surrounding them. He knows everything Tom says is true, but loving Zsuzsa feels like letting go of Karen. He's not sure if he can do that. Since he's known Zsuzsa, he's put her at risk twice. She'd be better off without him.

Chapter 53

Peter

Peter sits looking out the window of the streetcar. Night has fallen over Budapest and the lights sparkle. Tomorrow will be Christmas Eve, Peter's first since returning to Hungary. It's been thirty-eight years since he last celebrated Christmas here. When he was a child, December 5 meant more to him than December 24. Szent Miklós, the Hungarian equivalent of Santa Claus, would visit children on the fifth. On the twenty-fifth, baby Jesus would deliver gifts. Christmas Eve was just another day. Will it still be that way? He isn't sure.

Drawing closer to his stop, his thoughts shift to work. He's still in shock over the death of Kovacs. Thinking about it brings a feeling of loneliness. Kovacs was his link to the task force. He can't get over the shock of seeing Kovacs killed. He isn't sure if he ever will. What troubles him most is who was driving the car. It wasn't Toth. No way he would put himself in that kind of danger. Had he hired someone to kill Kovacs? Was he working with someone? Had Kovacs even been the target? Was his own life in danger now? So many questions abound.

The train conductor announces the next stop, the stop he's been waiting for. Peter stands and moves to the door, leaning against the railing as they glide toward the stop. His mind shifts back to a little over a year ago. In the weeks before his wife's death, he was working on a murder case that had been drug-related. While investigating, he found the murder weapon had been owned by a fellow police officer. The officer claimed that the gun had been stolen and he had neglected to report it missing. The officer was put on leave. While on leave, Peter had followed him to a house where a drug deal was taking place. Peter had pulled financial records on the officer and found nothing. But his wife had made several large cash deposits over the prior few months. Peter had planned to talk with the wife when his own wife had been murdered. Peter hadn't even considered the two cases could be related. Now he knew they probably were, and he didn't know how far up the chain the corruption went.

He feels the brakes engage on the streetcar as they slow to a stop. The doors open, and Peter steps out onto the sidewalk. Zsuzsa's apartment is only a block away, and he's grateful. It's even colder now than it was earlier. The temperatures have gone from brisk to frigid with the setting of the sun. He increases his pace, knowing Zsuzsa's company will warm him. After talking with Tom, their conversation has occupied his thoughts. Tom was right, again. He wasn't being fair to Zsuzsa. Tonight will be different. He'd relax. Let himself enjoy her company. The thought brings a spring to his step.

As he draws within a few paces of her building, he sees two police cars lined up along the sidewalk. In front of them is a black Volkswagen Passat. The Passat looks like the one he was driven home in from the hospital. As he reaches the front doors to the apartment building, a man steps out from beside the building and blocks Peter's path. He's flanked by two police officers on either side.

"Good evening, Peter." Peter looks into the eyes of Detective Szabo. The two officers come forward to stand on either side of Peter. "Andrassy Peter, you're under arrest for conspiracy to murder Detective Kovacs Lajos. You'll now be taken into custody."

Szabo indicates with a nod to the two police officers, and they take Peter by the shoulders, turning him around. His back is to Szabo. Peter knows there's little point in fighting. He accepts his fate. Szabo withdraws a set of handcuffs and wraps them around Peter's wrists, pinning his arms behind his back. The two officers then lead him to the police car, open the back door, and help him inside. As they drive away, Peter looks up and sees Zsuzsa watching from her window.

Epilogue

I'm not sure about this. I gaze into the mirror and don't love what I see. Something isn't right. Is it my hair? Makeup? I think it's my outfit. Peter didn't give me much to go on. We'll be going to dinner, but what else? Where will we be going? How fancy should I be? I look at the black dress I'm wearing. Is it too much? What else could I wear?

I walk out of my bathroom and back to the closet. I look up at the clothes hanging. I don't like any of the options. This dress is super cute, but it might be too sexy. A little too much fun. Peter is an older man; I might give him a heart attack. It's more of a cocktail dress than a dinner dress. But then again, maybe Peter will take me somewhere fancy. He does owe me, and I do look so good in this. It's cut a little low. He's going to have a hard time keeping his eyes off me.

I look across the room to the wall on the opposite side of the bed. It's seven o'clock. He should be here anytime. I slip on my matching set of pumps, twirl in the mirror once, and grab a matching black sweater deciding I can either leave it on or take it off depending on where we go. As I walk into the front room, I notice a chorus of red and blue lights flashing outside my window. That's weird. I walk to the window, pull back the curtain, and look out. Four men stand on the sidewalk beside my window. Two are policemen in uniform. One of the men is standing with his hands behind his back. The other guy pulls out a set of handcuffs. I think they're arresting him.

The two policemen turn the guy around. I look closer. I'd recognize those broad shoulders anywhere. It's Peter. What are they doing? Why are they arresting him? I knock on the windowpane.

"Peter! Peter!"

I'm too far up. He can't hear me. I think about running downstairs, but not in these heels and dress. Plus, I'm glued to the window. They grab him roughly and guide him to one of the police cars. They're taking him. The plain-clothes man shuts the door and turns, revealing his face. He looks familiar. Where do I know him? But just as I ask the question, I know the answer. I saw him in the club. Gin and tonic. I served him in there. Something isn't right. What could they be arresting Peter for?

The man gets into the front seat, and the car pulls away. My eyes focus on the back-seat window, and I see Peter push his face near the glass. He looks up at me. We lock eyes. In that instant, it's almost like I can read his thoughts. He needs my help.

I turn back to the closet and begin to undress. They've ruined our date, but they aren't taking Peter from me without a fight.

Also By

D.J. Maughan

Revealing the Shadows

Book Three in the Vanished Series

She warned him she was being followed, and now she's dead. If he finds her killer, will he end up the same way?

Peter Andrassy is tortured by guilt. Widowed for a year and looking for redemption, the former NYC detective is in a Budapest prison for a murder he didn't commit. His work with the national police has brought a new perspective. For the first time in months, he knows he can solve his wife's murder, but he might be too late.

His only ally in the Hungarian National Police is dead, and he's been accused of the murder. Every minute he remains locked up, the trafficking syndicate grows in power.

Can Peter escape prison and bring his wife's killer to justice?

Revealing the Shadows is the suspenseful third book in the Vanished series. You'll love D.J. Maughan's gripping thriller if you like unique characters, twisted plots, and determined detectives.

Buy *Revealing the Shadows* to immerse yourself in this page-turner today!

Vanished From Budapest
Book One in the Vanished Series
Two graduate students fall in love; one goes missing....

In the year 2000, Peter Andrassy is heartbroken by the murder of his wife. Widowed for a year and hoping to mend his broken heart, the former NYC detective has returned to his home country of Hungary to work as a private investigator when he's contacted by an American graduate student who is desperate to find his missing British girlfriend.

A gifted interrogator, Peter senses the boyfriend is intentionally withholding information. Could it be related to sex trafficking? Young women, often foreign, disappear daily in the capital city, never to be seen again. The clock is ticking, and the case is growing cold.

Can Peter find Samantha before it's too late?

Vanished From Budapest is the gripping first book in the Vanished series. If you like unique characters, intriguing settings, and hard-boiled detectives, then you'll love D.J. Maughan's page-turning abduction thriller.

Buy Vanished From Budapest to see if Samantha is indeed a victim of trafficking.

About Author

Thank you for reading my book. I know I've left you hanging. Remember, this is a series and there's a reason for it. Like you, I'm selective when it comes to books, and I'm humbled you chose mine. I'm an avid reader, event manager, father, public speaker, and author. I lived in Budapest as a younger man and have returned to visit multiple times. I hope you could feel my love for the city as you read the book. Hungary gave me the best education of my life, and I will always be grateful for my time there. Beyond reading six to eight books a month, I enjoy cooking, DIY projects at home, dinner with my wife, working out, playing basketball with my sons, watching live sports, and traveling. I seek inspiration everywhere, especially while studying and visiting diverse places and cultures. Whether jumping from a cliff in Hawaii or hiking the Plitvice Lakes in Croatia, I'm in heaven as long as my wife and four teenage boys are at my side.

Connect with me at http://djmaughan.com. Sign up for my newsletter and stay informed on forthcoming books and releases. I'll also offer you a free story, The Villains Mask. It's about Andras, the villain from book one.

If you enjoyed Pursuit of Demons, I'd appreciate a review and rating. No need for anything more than a sentence or two.